"Someone been trying to marry you off?" LeAnna asked.

At his nod, she continued. "You might not appreciate the interference. But the next time they try to match you up with someone, maybe you should go for it."

Vince didn't shrug his shoulders in an offhand way, as she'd expected. Instead, he stood statue-still, his hands on his hips, his eyes staring straight at her.

She pulled her gaze from his, letting it trail down the strong column of his throat, over his shoulders, all the way down to the newly painted red wagon at his knees—the wagon he'd brought as a gift for her son.

No, she thought, her attraction for this man didn't change anything. It didn't change the fact that she couldn't allow herself to get too close to him. If she did, she'd never want to leave. And she had to leave.

If she stayed, and if they were found, her life, and her child's, could very well come to an end.

Dear Reader,

Babies—who can resist them? Celebrating the wonder of new life—and new love—Silhouette Romance introduces a brand-new series, BUNDLES OF JOY. In these wonderful stories, couples are brought together by babies—and kept together by love! We hope you enjoy all six BUNDLES OF JOY books in April. Look for more in the months to come.

Favorite author Suzanne Carey launches the series with *The Daddy Project*. Sherry Tompkins is caring for her infant nephew and she needs help from the child's father, Mike Ruiz. Is marrying Mike the best way to find out if he's daddy material?

Lindsay Longford brings us *The Cowboy, the Baby and the Runaway Bride*. T. J. Tyler may have been left at the altar years ago by Callie Jo Murphy, but now this rugged cowboy and his adorable baby boy are determined to win her back.

Lullaby and Goodnight is a dramatic new story from Sandra Steffen about a single mom on the run. LeAnna Chadwick longs to stay in the shelter of Vince Macelli's arms, but the only way to protect her child is to leave the man she loves.

The excitement continues with *Adam's Vow*, Karen Rose Smith's book about one man's search for his missing daughters—and the beautiful, mysterious woman who helps him. Love and laughter abound in Pat Montana's *Babies Inc.*, a tale of two people who go into the baby business together and find romance in the process. And debut author Christine Scott brings us the heartwarming *Hazardous Husband*.

I hope you will enjoy BUNDLES OF JOY. Until next month—

Happy Reading!

Anne Canadeo
Senior Editor
Silhouette Romance

Please address questions and book requests to:
Silhouette Reader Service
U.S.: 3010 Walden Ave., P.O. Box 1325, Buffalo, NY 14269
Canadian: P.O. Box 609, Fort Erie, Ont. L2A 5X3

LULLABY AND GOODNIGHT

Sandra Steffen

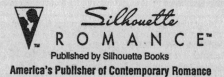

Silhouette
ROMANCE™
Published by Silhouette Books
America's Publisher of Contemporary Romance

For Rose, Diane, Nancy and Carol—
My brothers had the good sense to marry you.
I've had the good fortune to be your friend.

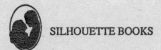 SILHOUETTE BOOKS

ISBN 0-373-19074-3

LULLABY AND GOODNIGHT

Copyright © 1995 by Sandra E. Steffen

This edition published by arrangement with Harlequin Enterprises B.V.

Printed in U.S.A.

SANDRA STEFFEN

Creating memorable characters is one of Sandra's favorite aspects of writing. She's always been a romantic, and is thrilled to be able to spend her days doing what she loves—bringing her characters to life on her computer screen.

Sandra grew up in Michigan, the fourth of ten children, all of whom have taken the old adage "Go forth and multiply" quite literally. Add to this her husband, who is her real-life hero, their four school-age sons who keep their lives in constant motion, their gigantic cat, Percy, and her wonderful friends, in-laws and neighbors, and what do you get? Chaos, of course, but also a wonderful sense of belonging she wouldn't trade for the world.

Dear Readers,

When I was given the opportunity to tell you how I feel about children, I wasn't sure whether I'd need twenty pages or only three words: I adore them. Okay, four words: I really adore them. I might need those twenty pages after all....

I loved each of our four bundles of joy to distraction months before I counted their little fingers and toes or looked into their trusting blue eyes. The terrible two's? Nah. I've always thought they should be called the independent two's. "Just wait until they're teenagers," people used to say. Greg, Doug, Brad and Mike are all teenagers now, and I still love them to distraction.

Size thirteen shoes have taken the place of little blue booties, and the sounds coming from stereos waft down the stairs instead of crying. Bottles and diapers no longer fill every available space in our house. Instead, there are basketballs and baseballs, Garfield clocks and posters of people who barely look human.

I love the noise, the whirlwind of activity, the conversation and the laughter. I can't imagine my life without children; I can't imagine my books without them, either. That's why I'm so pleased to present *Lullaby and Goodnight* to you as part of Silhouette's BUNDLES OF JOY series. There's a bit of my boys in Casey, and a bit of myself in this story. So, whether you have kids of your own, hope to someday or will simply always be just a kid at heart, I wish you all of life's best.

Sincerely,

Sandra Steffen

Chapter One

The truck was heading right for her, and it didn't look like it was going to stop. LeAnna gripped her steering wheel with both hands, frantically searching the highway for some place to go, some way to avoid the imminent collision.

The blare of a horn nearly obliterated the squeal of tires, but nothing could cover the fear that threatened to paralyze her as the out-of-control vehicle skidded straight for her passenger door. Jamming the brake pedal to the floor, she cried, "Hold on, Casey."

The toddler's head jerked to the back of his car seat, and he let out a strangled cry. The pickup's bumper ground into her front fender, the impact propelling both vehicles into the median, where they finally came to a grinding stop.

"Mama!" Casey cried.

It required all LeAnna's strength to pry her fingers from the steering wheel and steady her hands as she reached out to comfort Casey and make sure he was unharmed. She

touched her palm to his face, and he pressed his little cheek
into her hand in a way that nearly broke her heart.

"It's all right," she crooned. "I'm here. It's all right. I'm
going to keep you safe, sweetheart. I promise. I promise."

At her words and her touch, his whimpers quieted. She
didn't remember unfastening her seat belt, but she doubted
she'd ever forget the trust in the baby-brown eyes staring
into her own. Love for this beautiful child swelled in her
heart, and she fought to control the lump rising to her
throat.

The passenger door was pulled open. Over the din of the
truck's horn, a policeman shouted, "Are either of you
hurt?"

LeAnna's gaze swept upward, over the man's uniform,
until she found herself gazing into another pair of dark
brown eyes. Unlike Casey's, these eyes weren't filled with
trust. An instinctive warning washed over her at the thor-
oughness of the police officer's gaze.

"Are you hurt?" he repeated.

She didn't try to shout over the noise. With Casey safe in
her arms, she simply shook her head and tramped down her
unease, telling herself this man couldn't possibly know
anything about her.

His eyes narrowed, and the muscles in his jaw clenched.
Casting a look toward the pickup, he muttered something
under his breath and strode around the front of her car to
jerk the other vehicle's hood up and yank out a wire. An
instant later, the blaring horn trailed away.

"Whuzat?"

LeAnna followed the direction of Casey's chubby finger.
"That's a police car," she answered.

"Whuzat?" he asked again, pointing at the policeman
striding toward them.

Before she could answer, the officer spoke. "I'm Officer
Macelli. If you're sure you and your baby are all right, I'm

going to need to see your driver's license, the car's registration, and your proof of insurance.''

A middle-aged man with a hardy paunch chimed in. ''I saw the whole thing, Vince, and this little lady didn't do anything wrong. The other driver barreled right through the stop sign, and on into her car.''

LeAnna noticed that a few other spectators had gathered, and in the confusion that followed, she realized that it didn't matter whose fault the accident had been. An accident report would be filed. And she could be traced here.

Vince Macelli let out one deep breath and took another. He'd been on his way back to the station three blocks away when he heard the first squeal of tires. His adrenaline had kicked into high gear, and by the time he heard the crash, he'd already been pulling out of a U-turn and heading back toward the highway. The accident hadn't been as serious as he'd feared, and by now his breathing should have returned to normal.

Everything he'd done had been pretty much routine, from directing traffic around the accident, to taking everyone's statements and license numbers, to issuing a ticket to the driver of the pickup truck. But there was nothing routine about the way his eyes kept straying to the woman with the chestnut-colored hair curling to her shoulders. And there was certainly nothing routine about the way he felt when she met his gaze.

According to her driver's license, LeAnna Chadwick was only twenty-six years old. But there was something in her wide brown eyes that made her seem older in a way that had nothing to do with actual years.

With her purse on one shoulder and two suitcases and a diaper bag at her feet, she watched until the wrecker towing her car had disappeared around the corner. Her baby was getting cranky, and Vince was surprised at the protective instincts that surfaced as he watched her struggle with her child. He couldn't help noticing the way her voice shook as she tried to soothe the baby's tears, or the way her lips moved when she pressed a kiss to the top of his head.

"Is there someone you want to call?" he asked. "Your husband, maybe?"

She took a deep breath and shifted the baby to her other hip. "No. There's no one."

"Not even a friend?"

She was obviously weighing his question, and for a moment he wondered if she intended to answer him at all. When she did, it wasn't with words, but with a firm shake of her head.

"Come on, then," Vince said, reaching for her suitcases. "I'll drive you to a motel."

He stashed her cases in the backseat and held the passenger door for her. Hesitating, she glanced into the car. Vince had the distinct impression that climbing into a police car was the last thing she wanted to do.

She swung around to face him, her full skirt brushing his pant leg. "I don't see a car seat," she murmured. "You won't arrest me for not putting Casey in one, will you?"

He'd been trying so hard to place her accent, it took him a moment to recognize the sparkle in her eyes for what it was. Fine-witted humor. Vince felt a burning deep in his chest, and realized it was from lack of oxygen. This woman took his breath away. Literally.

Evidently she'd seen the Buckle Up—It's the Law signs on her way through the state. He wondered where she was headed, and spent longer than he should on that thought. Her car had a Tennessee license plate, but her accent wasn't what he'd call southern. It wasn't midwestern, either, so Vince doubted she was from Michigan.

"Is everything all right, Officer?" she asked, drawing his gaze.

Her wit had snuck up on him, but not as much as the little smile lifting her lips. He'd been attracted to her the first moment he saw her, had had a hard enough time keeping a clear head when she'd barely looked his way, when he'd thought she was married. Now that he knew she wasn't, the possibilities seemed endless. For now, he had to get himself under control, or that smile of hers was going to be his undoing.

"Everything's fine, and under the circumstances, I wouldn't dream of arresting you," he replied, in a lazily seductive tone he barely recognized as his own.

So much for getting himself under control. He hadn't come right out and said what he *would* dream of doing with her, but he might as well have, because it was there in his voice. He knew it, and the way her eyes widened told him she did, too.

He took a quick, sharp breath, telling himself it wasn't too late to find the line of professionalism and step back behind it. He closed her door and stalked around to the driver's side of the police car, intending to do just that. After settling himself behind the steering wheel he said, "There are three small motels here in Millerton. One in practically every direction."

She seemed to give the information careful consideration before saying, "Would you take us to the least expensive one?"

The least expensive motel was on the northern outskirts of town. He'd been inside the place a few times when he was a kid. It had been drafty, dirty, and mouse-infested then. He'd been called out there a month ago to settle a dispute between two old rivals who'd had too much to drink. The place hadn't changed, at least not for the better. Although he knew it was none of his business, he hated the thought of LeAnna Chadwick and her son staying there. Even for one night.

"That would be the Grady Motel. But I wouldn't recommend it. Millerton's a small city, but it has made it into the twentieth century—now that it's almost over—and if money's a problem, the other two motels both accept credit cards."

"I don't use credit cards," she replied evenly.

Vince thought that was a little unusual in this day and age, but kept his opinion to himself, and cast a quick glance her way. She was looking straight ahead, her chin resting on top of the baby's curly head. Her lips were full, her mouth was narrow. Her face was oval-shaped, and Vince had to fight the urge to smooth three errant curls away from her eyes. There were no lines in her gold-toned skin, and there was certainly no gray in her auburn hair. Yet, even in profile, she seemed far too weary for someone her age.

"How bad is that motel?" she asked. "I mean, as long as it's safe, it'll be all right. All Casey and I need is a place to spend the night while my car is being fixed."

Vince didn't know why he turned left at the next corner. He sure as heck didn't know why he cared one way or the other where LeAnna Chadwick and her baby spent the night. But he did care, and he didn't want to analyze it, not here, not now.

With her arms wrapped around Casey, LeAnna watched the scenery go by. The dark, brooding policeman had taken the last corner a little fast. Even as she steadied Casey, worry prickled down her spine. He'd said the Grady Motel was on the north end of town. They were heading west.

"Where are we going?"

LeAnna heard the quiet desperation in her own voice and felt a rising panic. She instinctively memorized a street sign, and cast a look at the man beside her.

His mouth was set in a grim line, and his jaw was clenched in a way that scared her. He took his eyes from the street long enough to look at her, and her fear sailed to the other side of the sun. His eyes were a clear dark brown and bespoke an innate intelligence and independence of spirit, an unusual blend, considering the arrogant set of his shoulders and the tough-boy jut of his chin.

She believed the eyes were a window to the soul, and over the past several years she'd learned to trust what she saw in those windows. There was anger in this man's eyes, and the hint of a temper, even a little bit of male appreciation. But no evil.

A muscle moved in his jaw, and LeAnna lowered her eyes. Better not let him see too far into *her* soul.

"I didn't mean to scare you," he began. "I thought of a place you can stay."

He was trying to be kind to her, trying to put her mind at ease. If it had been any other time and place, she would have reached her hand out to him, letting him know she appreciated his efforts. But this wasn't another time and place. This was here and now, and right now all LeAnna should be thinking about was finding a place to spend the night.

"Another motel?" she asked.

He shook his head, pulling the police car into a narrow driveway. "I moved into a new house a month ago. You can spend the night in the old one, free of charge."

In order to view the house, LeAnna had to look past the clear-cut lines of his profile, past the firm jawline, beard-shadowed cheek and long straight nose. The house was a white-sided story-and-a-half. It was plain and old, but not run-down. The lawn was mowed, the trim painted. The front steps looked relatively new. But there was no lamp in the front window, and she didn't see a shrub or flowering bush anywhere. The place looked well kept, but not well loved.

"How long did you live here?" she asked.

"Most of my life."

That simple statement said more than a hundred words could have. LeAnna remembered her grandmother proudly spouting, "Home is where the heart is." There seemed to be very little of Officer Macelli's heart here.

"Is it empty?" she asked, not certain whether she was referring to his house or his heart.

That thought brought LeAnna to her senses. Her life was a shambles, and had been even before that man ran a stop sign and crashed into her car. She needed to find a job, and a place for her and Casey to live. A place that was safe. She had no business thinking about this man's heart, and no time to think about hers.

Casey began to squirm on her lap, and LeAnna reached into the diaper bag near her feet for a cracker. It was after six o'clock. Casey would be wanting supper, and they both needed a good night's sleep. Suddenly the plain white house looked incredibly inviting.

"Come on inside," Officer Macelli said, "and I'll show you around."

He reached for her suitcases, and LeAnna followed him across the side yard, automatically noting an old white-washed garage at the end of the driveway and a couple of gnarled old trees out back. Moments later, she stepped into a rectangular kitchen. Like the outside, the house's interior was clean and tidy, and completely devoid of anything remotely homey.

She set Casey on his feet and prepared to follow him as he toddled away to investigate his new surroundings. Behind her, she heard a series of clicks, followed by footsteps, as Officer Macelli strode to the other side of the kitchen, where he flicked another switch, casting the room in artificial brightness.

From the doorway he said, "I hauled most of the furniture to the dump before I moved into my new place. I haven't decided whether to sell this house or rent it out, so I left the old sofa, a table and chairs, and a bed."

Casey made a beeline for the diaper bag lying near the door. LeAnna beat him there, offering him a small pack of raisins. She cast a sweeping glance at the austere kitchen and said, "This house will be fine for the night. I appreciate you letting us stay here, Officer."

"No problem," he said, inclining his head toward the next room. "The bathroom's through that door. The next room is the living room. Beyond that are two small bedrooms. And you might as well call me Vince, since you'll be sleeping in my bed tonight."

She jerked her head up and found him watching her, his gaze steady. For a moment, his eyes darkened with a curious intensity. Only a fool could have pretended she didn't respond to the private message in his eyes. And LeAnna Chadwick was no fool.

Her gaze instinctively sought Casey's whereabouts, her consciousness instinctively warning her against openly admitting to a mutual attraction. She heard Vince clear his throat, but with weariness washing over her, she couldn't bring herself to meet his gaze again.

He strode to the door. By the time he'd turned toward her again, she'd straightened her spine, her emotions under control.

"Thanks again," she said matter-of-factly. "I really do appreciate your kindness."

"LeAnna?"

She met his gaze, breathing through parted lips. Waiting. For what, she wasn't sure.

By no means was she blind to his attraction. By no means did she have any intention of acting on it. With his implication that they should be on a first-name basis because she'd be sleeping in his bed hanging between them, she half expected him to make a suggestive comment.

Instead, he said, "You've had a bad day."

She nodded. She'd had worse.

She saw a muscle clench in his jaw, but he didn't question her silence. "The wrecker took your car to O'Malley's. They should have an estimate for you in the morning. In the meantime, try to get some sleep."

Seconds later, he was gone. She closed the door behind him, locking it securely, but it was a long time before her heart rate returned to normal.

Casey began to whine, and she bustled about, changing his diaper, searching through her cases for something that would pass for supper. She opened the window to let in some fresh air, and spotted the perfect place to relax. With Casey on one hip and everything else they'd need in her other hand, she slipped out the back door.

"Whuzat?" Casey asked after popping another piece of cereal into his mouth.

"That," LeAnna answered with a grin, "is an ant."

"Ont," Casey repeated, immediately searching for something else to point to.

LeAnna handed him his box of juice, hoping to momentarily divert his attention to his supper. The ploy worked. For the next several minutes, he sat next to her on the back stoop, a plastic bowl tucked between his legs, a slice of cheese in one hand, his cardboard box of juice on the cement stoop beside him.

After taking a sip of her own juice, LeAnna let her head fall back. She could see the colors of light through her eyelids, glowing shades of yellow, orange and red. She imagined she could feel those colors in the warmth of the sun's rays, heating her face, her hair, and her body. For a moment, her guard was down, and she imagined she was on the mountain, safe and secure.

"Whuzat?"

She felt a smile steal across her face at Casey's question, and brought her head back down, expecting him to be pointing to a new green leaf or a blade of grass. Instead, he was pointing at a reed-thin woman with steel-gray hair, a woman who was hurrying toward them, carrying a tray.

"Evenin'," she called. "Name's Loretta Trierweller, but everybody 'round here calls me Lettie. I live next door, and I thought you and the little one might be hungry, so I fixed up this here tray for the both of you."

LeAnna breathed in the aroma of hot food, hungrily eyeing the items on the tray. "It's been a long time since I've had homemade macaroni and cheese."

"Well, it's high time you tried some of mine, then. Here," she said, pushing one plate toward LeAnna. "You go ahead and eat, and I'll help the baby."

Casey jerked backward, out of Lettie's reach. In his haste to climb onto LeAnna's lap, he kicked his drink, and the box toppled over onto the ground. Clutching LeAnna with all his might, he buried his face in her neck without making a sound.

LeAnna wrapped her arms around him, murmuring soft words in his ear. Casting a glance at the other woman to gauge her reaction, she whispered, "He's overtired."

"Who wouldn't be, considering what he's been through?" Lettie countered.

LeAnna fought her clamoring nerves. How could this woman possibly know what Casey had been through?

Either Lettie Trierweller didn't notice the way LeAnna's hand suddenly shook along Casey's back, or she wasn't expecting a two-sided conversation. She prattled on, asking questions and, more often than not, answering those same questions herself.

"Of course he's tired, and probably wound up after that accident and all. I'll bet he's a little on the shy side, too, so

I'll just sit way over here, out of his way, until he warms up some."

As if he realized this woman wasn't a threat after all, Casey gradually relaxed and allowed LeAnna to sit him down next to Lettie. He drew the line at letting her feed him. Holding the fork in one chubby little hand, he ate with the other.

"Land sakes," Lettie declared. "It looks like it's a good thing I brought along these clean towels."

LeAnna glanced at the linens folded over the other woman's arm. As casually as she could manage, she asked, "How did you know we'd be needing those?"

"Vince called and told me. Said you were staying the night here, and what with him living in his new house and all, he wondered if I'd mind bringing a few things over to make your stay more comfortable."

LeAnna and Casey ate on, the home-cooked meal and Lettie's constant chattering a calming balm to them both.

"Hope you don't mind my talkin'. My Bud always says I talk a mile a minute. It's just so nice to have a woman to talk to, that's all."

"I don't mind at all," LeAnna declared truthfully.

Lettie rambled on, and in a relatively short amount of time, LeAnna had gleaned a lot of information. For instance, she now knew that May was Lettie's favorite month of the year and that Millerton had an equal number of churches and fast-food places, one *decent* sit-down restaurant, and the Millerton Diner.

"My sister, Trudy, owns the diner, and let me tell you, if you ever want to know what's going on in this town, ask her. She can tell you who's getting married, who's pregnant, and who's been promoted to foreman down at the plant."

LeAnna smiled as she bit into an oatmeal cookie.

"Shoot, Trudy probably knows what Rusty got on his algebra test before Bud or I do. Rusty's our fifteen-year-old grandson, and he's been livin' with us for close to two years now. Got in trouble with a gang in Detroit. Got in trouble here, too, until Vince straightened him out some.''

Keeping Casey, who had toddled off to investigate the backyard, in her line of vision, LeAnna listened to every word Lettie said. She was curious about Vince Macelli, and would have liked to ask questions. But a person asking questions tended to draw attention, and LeAnna knew it would be best if she and Casey weren't remembered when they left.

''Don't know what Bud and I woulda done if Vince hadn't talked to the boy. Not that we deserved Vince's help. Ever wish you could go back and change the past, Le-Anna?''

LeAnna let the question soak into her mind the way Casey's drink had soaked into the ground below. With her gaze trained on Casey, she said, ''Yes, Lettie, I have wished I could change the past. If I could, I'd do a lot of things differently.''

But she wouldn't change the fact that Casey John Chadwick trusted her. She vowed to do anything to keep him safe.

Lettie nodded her head vigorously. ''If I had it to do all over again, I'd be a better mother to my Dolores, and maybe she wouldn't have run off and gotten married when she was only seventeen. But then we wouldn't have Rusty. Having him is one thing I wouldn't change.''

Following Casey's progress across the backyard, Le-Anna felt a lump form in her throat. If she could have found her voice, she'd have told Lettie she knew exactly how she felt. LeAnna wouldn't change the fact that she had Casey, either.

Lettie was talking again. ''Never made no sense to me, the way LeRoy treated Vince. If I hadn't been so busy worrying about Dolores, and making ends meet, and Bud's drinking problem, I woulda been kinder to that boy. His mother

tried, but she had her own troubles. Still, I remember how
LeRoy Macelli's voice used to carry over here in the summer, how he used to yell at the boy. One time I saw LeRoy
raise his fist to Vince. Vince musta been around twelve or so.
He was tall for his age, but little-boy wiry, ya know? Anyway, I'll never forget the rage in LeRoy's shaking fist, or the
way Vince took the blow that followed. He took it, he did.
Without flinching.''

A tear rolled down LeAnna's cheek. Rather than brush it
away with her fingertips, she raised her head to the sky, letting the moisture evaporate in the warm evening breeze.

Lettie left a short time later, calling a goodbye to Casey,
then disappearing to the other side of the hedge. LeAnna
took Casey inside, unable to get Lettie's words out of her
mind. Over and over, the image of a young Vince Macelli
facing his father's angry fist shimmered through her
thoughts.

Later, kneeling on the floor next to the old tub, she gave
Casey a bath, laughing as he played. Luckily, Casey didn't
seem to notice that her laughter was hollow.

LeAnna's sock-clad feet didn't make a sound as she pad-
ded to the kitchen. It was only eleven o'clock, but every
house in the neighborhood was already dark. Casey was
sound asleep, and she knew she should be, too.

She'd driven during most of the previous night, and during Casey's nap this afternoon. Since her little boy wasn't a
very good passenger, she'd found it worked best to drive
while he slept. Now she was exhausted, but too keyed up to
rest.

After Casey's bath, he had toddled from one end of the
nearly empty house to the other. But it hadn't been long
before the home-cooked meal and the long, hot bath worked
their magic on him. Relaxed, clean and well-fed, he'd
dropped off to sleep earlier than usual.

LeAnna seized the first real privacy she'd had in a long, long time. She soaked in the tub, lathering the washcloth with the soap Lettie had given her and smoothing it over her skin. Being careful to use only a small amount of the shampoo she'd taken from her purse, she washed and rinsed her long hair.

Almost an hour later, she stepped from the bath, wrapped in Lettie's towel. Taking a pair of soft white sweats from her suitcase, she pulled them up her bare legs and shrugged into an oversize black T-shirt, then proceeded to comb the tangles from her wet hair. Before closing her suitcase, she ran her hand over the letter tucked safely beneath her clothes. She didn't have to remove the stationery from its envelope; she'd memorized every word. She closed her eyes, trying not to give in to the futile wish that things could be different. Taking a deep breath, she strode from the room, intent upon investigating her new surroundings.

At first LeAnna relished the quiet, the solitude, the freedom to roam an entire house late at night. Standing at the kitchen sink, she washed the clothes she and Casey had worn that day and hung them over the shower rod to dry. She wasn't sure when the solitude turned into loneliness, but she did her best to ignore it.

She continued to wander through the house, counting windows instead of sheep. Counting heat registers and floor tiles, light switches and electrical outlets. There were eight windows in all, and four registers for heat, five light switches and ten electrical outlets. She'd lost track of the floor tiles somewhere after eighty-nine.

Ah, counting was helping her relax, helping keep her mind off the crazed look in Nick's eyes the last time she'd seen him. Counting always helped.

She counted four kitchen drawers, and three kitchen cupboards. There was one door in the living room, another one leading to the side yard, and one more facing the backyard. Three doors. That seemed like a lot for a house this size. But they were all locked, safe and secure.

LeAnna rotated her neck in half circles, and felt a huge yawn pull at her mouth, making her drowsy. Sleep wasn't far away now.

She turned off the kitchen light, and slowly made her way into the living room, unconsciously counting each footstep. She stood at the dark window and yawned again.

The three-quarter moon cast shadows across the front yard. There was a streetlight down on the corner, but it wasn't powerful enough to reach this far. Somewhere, a dog barked. Otherwise, the neighborhood was completely quiet. Slowly LeAnna turned away from the window, the moonlight all she needed to make her way to the second door.

A scrape of metal stopped her footsteps.

Her ears strained for another sound. Another came. From the kitchen.

She'd locked the door. She knew she had. Fear snaked down her spine. Millerton had seemed like a small peaceful town, but LeAnna knew better than anyone that evil could happen anywhere.

The door creaked open.

Bringing her fisted hands to her throat, LeAnna tried to remain calm. Casey was sound asleep in the bedroom. Safe, for the moment. She pressed her back to the living room wall, frantically searching her mind for the location of an object, an ashtray or flowerpot, anything she could use in self-defense. In her mind she saw each stark room, devoid of all but the barest pieces of furniture.

The door creaked as it was opened farther, and fear filled her chest. She had no weapon. All she had was her intelligence, her speed, and the element of surprise.

LeAnna tramped down the panic threatening to choke her. Silently she crept closer to the doorway. And waited.

Chapter Two

The fresh air streaming through the open door did nothing to relieve the burning in LeAnna's lungs. She pressed her back to the wall, listening for the smallest sound from the next room. She heard a click, and the crinkle of plastic. Seconds later, there was another faint sound, like the sleeve of a jacket brushing against the wall.

LeAnna moved around to the other side of the doorway, praying the floor wouldn't creak. Even when the old floor tiles didn't betray her, she was careful letting out her breath. Her hand came into contact with a smooth rail, and she knew she'd reached her destination.

Her blood pounded in her ears, making her strong. With the element of surprise on her side, she'd have a fighting chance of outmaneuvering the intruder.

She grasped the old metal-and-vinyl chair with one hand and felt behind her with the other. She flicked on the light switch and swung into action. Squinting against the sudden brightness, she raised the chair like a club, ready to strike.

"LeAnna!"

The flashes in her vision receded, and her eyes focused.

Vince Macelli swore.

So did LeAnna.

With her heart beating in her throat, she rasped out, "Vince! You almost scared me half to death."

"You almost scared me twice that much," he cut in. A vein pulsed in his neck, and his whole demeanor was sharp and severe.

Now that the surge of adrenaline was over, the chair she held upside down at shoulder level was getting awfully heavy. She lowered it to the floor with jerky movements, but didn't remove her hands from its back.

"What are you doing here?"

Vince heard the tremor of fear in her voice, and saw it in the white-knuckled grip she had on the back of the chair. She'd thought he was an intruder. She'd been terrified, yet she hadn't cowered in fear. Even with surprise and anger fighting for space in his chest, he was moved by her courage.

She'd called him Vince. Not Officer Macelli. But Vince. The realization moved him in other ways.

Her hair was a riot of curls, and her eyes were like summer lightning. He didn't know anything about her, except that she was beautiful and brave. If the brushes of darkness beneath her eyes were any indication, she was also exhausted.

Trying for an even tone, he lifted the blankets in his hands. "The house was dark, and rather than disturb you, I thought I'd tiptoe in and leave a few things you might need, like blankets and milk. I know Lettie was by earlier, when I was still on duty, but I thought of a few other essentials that might come in handy." Without waiting for her to comment, he strode past her toward the bedroom. "You're tired. I'll just put these on the bed and let you get some sleep."

"That isn't necessary," she called to his back.

"No problem," he answered, shouldering through the doorway of the room he'd slept in most of his life.

His eyes took in the bare mattress and the little form huddled on the floor. Even in the semidarkness, Vince could see that the old quilt he'd left on the bed was now folded several times, making a soft cushion beneath the child sleeping on the threadbare carpet near the foot of the bed. A T-shirt had been used as a blanket, lovingly tucked around the sleeping child.

LeAnna stood directly behind him. The light from the living room threw their shadows onto the opposite wall, making them look larger than life and as out of proportion as a two-headed monster.

"Is he a light sleeper?" Vince whispered.

Vince saw the shake of her head in her shadow, and heard the velvet-edged emotion in her answering whisper. "Once he's asleep, a train could chug through the room, and I doubt he'd wake up."

Vince walked into the room, lowering the blankets and sheets stacked in his arms to the bed. LeAnna might claim the blankets hadn't been necessary, but he wondered how she'd have kept warm if he hadn't brought them. He cast a final glance around his old room, at the cold, bare bed, and at the child sleeping on the floor, safe and warm. With humbling clarity, he realized how much LeAnna Chadwick sacrificed for her child.

His own mother had made similar sacrifices for him.

Turning, he met LeAnna's eyes in the semidarkness. She was standing at an angle, the light behind her outlining the curve of her cheekbone and the shape of one breast. A surge of wanting streaked through him, a wanting that had nothing to do with reason.

As if she suddenly realized they were standing in his bedroom, she lowered her gaze and took a backward step. Without a sound, she turned in the doorway and strode toward the kitchen. Vince took a moment to run his hand over his eyes, another to take a deep breath and get his thoughts under control.

She was looking out the side window when he entered the kitchen. Without turning, she said, "Your car isn't in the driveway, and I didn't see it along the street. Where did you park?"

"I didn't. I only live two blocks away, and since it's a nice night, I decided to walk on over. I'm sorry I scared you, LeAnna."

She turned, finally meeting his gaze. Vince stayed where he was, in the kitchen doorway; she stayed where she was, at the window across the room. Although at least a dozen feet separated them, something passed between their gazes. Something unspoken, unbidden, powerful.

She was the first to look away.

His gaze slid down her, over the faded black T-shirt, which looked a size too big, down the white knit pants that stopped several inches above her ankles, and over the yellowed crew socks she wore on her feet. Her clothes didn't fit her very well. It was as if they'd been purchased secondhand. With his blood pumping through his veins, the significance of that impression was momentarily lost. The significance of the way his body reacted to this woman wasn't.

His gaze continued to roam across the floor, stopping on the bag he'd placed near the door when he first arrived, the bag he'd dropped moments before she flicked on the light and nearly clobbered him with his own kitchen chair. This was one woman he wouldn't want to tangle with in a dark alley. In a dark bedroom was a different story.

He tipped his head one time, gesturing toward the sack on the floor. "I put together a few things I thought you might need first thing in the morning. A teakettle and mug, and some instant coffee. I don't know what your baby eats for breakfast, but I thought he might want milk, so I brought over what was left of a half gallon."

He walked toward her, past her, and reached down for the sack. The plastic crinkled, and LeAnna realized it was the same sound she'd heard in the dark when he first entered the kitchen, when she thought he was someone else.

"You'll probably want to keep this cold." He opened the refrigerator and reached inside to turn it on before placing the container of milk on the top shelf.

He lifted the sack to the counter, but left the rest of the items inside. He was still looking at her, and she was at a loss for something to say. Seizing the first subject that came to mind, she said, "It was nice of you to bring those blankets. The milk and coffee, too."

His gaze didn't stray from hers as he said, "Just being neighborly."

"That's what the sign on the edge of town said."

He narrowed his eyes. "The sign?"

They were both still standing, but the atmosphere in the room had changed. LeAnna no longer had to grasp the back of the chair for support, and Vince casually leaned one shoulder against the refrigerator. Now that he was off duty, he wore jeans and a navy T-shirt instead of his police uniform. With one hand on his hip and the other in one pocket, he was the epitome of pure masculine brawn. Pure masculine brawn was one thing LeAnna would be wise to ignore.

Keeping her mind as clear and cool as ice water she said, "There's a sign outside of town that says Welcome to Neighborly Millerton—Population 5,078. Two minutes after I read it, that pickup truck smashed into me."

His mouth lifted in a small smile. She felt hers doing the same.

She continued, but the tone of her voice had warmed at least ten degrees. "I've seen a lot of city-limit signs, signs proclaiming their towns as historic or friendly. Millerton's the only one I've seen that says it's *neighborly.*"

"Sounds like you've been doing a lot of traveling. Where's home?"

This time LeAnna didn't say the first thing that came to mind. She carefully considered her answer before replying. "I grew up in the Smoky Mountains. But I haven't considered them home for a long time."

He nodded slowly. "And what brings you to Michigan?"

Again she considered her answer before speaking. "A friend of mine told me about a job south of here. I'm on my way there."

"That *neighborly* little accident altered your plans, huh?"

"Temporarily. But as long as they can have my car fixed by tomorrow, I'll be fine."

"So you're just passing through."

He was still leaning against the refrigerator, looking for all the world as if he belonged there. The dark brown eyes staring into hers were gentle, contemplative. For a moment LeAnna studied his face, unhurriedly, wishing they had more than this moment together. But she didn't have the luxury of time, and it would be best for everyone if she kept that in mind.

Nodding once, she said, "'Just passing through' sums it up pretty accurately."

Her words broke the spell between them. Vince straightened, his sudden movement jostling the grocery sack behind him. He righted the sack, then strode toward the side door.

"I jotted down the number to O'Malley's car repair. The phone here's been disconnected, but I'm sure Lettie would let you use hers if you asked."

At the door, he turned and cast her one last look. She didn't say goodbye. Neither did he.

After she'd closed the door behind him and locked it, after she'd removed the items from the grocery sack, after she'd done everything she could think to do, she wished she had at least thanked him. For the milk, the packets of instant oatmeal, the plastic spoons and bowls. She wished she'd thanked him for the blankets, and for the roof over her and Casey's head.

Even if she had thanked him, she couldn't have brought herself to say goodbye. Saying goodbye would have underlined the fact that tomorrow she'd be leaving, and would never get to know him better. She knew she couldn't allow herself to get to know anyone better. Especially not a policeman, a man who'd taken an oath to uphold the law.

LeAnna was no stranger to wishing. She'd spent most of her life wishing things could be different. This was one thing that had to be. Maybe someday things would change. For now, she had to concentrate on the present and the immediate future. Tonight she'd get a good night's sleep. Tomorrow she'd pick up her car and quietly drive out of town.

LeAnna was aware of Lettie's movements at the kitchen sink, just as she was aware that the older woman was listening to every word she said. "Yes, Mr. O'Malley. I understand."

She shifted Casey to her other hip, shifting the phone to her other ear. It took everything she had to keep the disappointment she felt deep inside from cracking her voice. "Four hundred twelve dollars, you say?"

Tom O'Malley rattled off the fees for fixing her car, and LeAnna mentally added up the money she had in her purse.

She'd started out with little money, and what she hadn't spent on food, diapers and lodging didn't come close to being enough to pay for the repairs to her car.

"Is there any way you can make it drivable without fixing the rest?" she asked.

The mechanic launched into another lengthy explanation, but the bottom line was no. The accident had left the front fender pushed in all the way to the wheel, making driving impossible. Not only would the fender have to be pulled out, but there was something wrong with the axle. She'd also need a new wheel and a new tire, because the wheel was damaged, and the old tire had a tear in it big enough to "throw a cat through," however big that was.

While the man rambled on about his trustworthy help, LeAnna felt her opportunity to make it to Lansing before five o'clock evaporate into thin air. Although the job at the privately owned day care wouldn't pay a lot, it included a room for her and Casey to stay in. That meant she could keep Casey with her all the time. It also meant she could save nearly every dollar she earned.

"The news ain't good, is it?" Lettie asked.

Shaking her head, LeAnna hung up the phone and took a deep breath. Casey was wiggling to get down, and LeAnna leaned over to set him on his feet. "There's a job waiting for me in . . . a town south of here, but only if I can be there this afternoon. Lettie, is there a bus stop in Millerton?"

"I'm afraid not. But I could give you a ride, if it's that important," Lettie declared.

LeAnna was touched by the offer, and mentally weighed her options. If she accepted Lettie's ride, she could take the job. But her car would still be here. That meant she'd have to depend on someone else to bring her back. She'd done that five months ago in Kentucky. Lonely and worried, she'd confided in a woman she'd thought was trustworthy.

The woman had seen it as a golden opportunity, and had contacted Nick. It had almost cost LeAnna everything. No, she had to depend on no one but herself.

Having reached her decision, she realized Lettie was talking. "If it's a job you're looking for, my sister Trudy could use another waitress at the diner."

Lettie handed Casey several measuring spoons, and LeAnna watched as he placed them, one by one, on the seat of a kitchen chair. At eighteen months, he was starting to talk, and if she wasn't mistaken, he was pretending to count those spoons. She thought she'd have become accustomed to the surge of emotions he felt at moments like these, when love threatened to fill her heart to the point of bursting. She'd do anything for her baby. Right now, that meant finding a job.

"What kind of people eat at the diner, Lettie?"

For a moment Lettie stared deep into LeAnna's eyes. "You aren't gonna make a lot in tips, that's for sure, but you aren't gonna have to fight off unwanted advances, either. In the morning the local folks come in for coffee and eggs and the latest gossip. Around noon they stop by for a hot lunch, or maybe a piece of Trudy's pie. There's a small supper crowd, too. But always local people. Men on business, or families on vacation, stop at the fast-food places along the highway."

To LeAnna's ears, that sounded safe. "Do you think your sister would hire me?"

Lettie's mouth widened into a conniving grin. "It just so happens that that sister of mine owes me a favor. You just leave Trudy to me."

Ten minutes later, Lettie hung up the phone in her old-fashioned kitchen, grinning from ear to ear. "You're in. She wants you to stop by this afternoon after the lunch crowd thins. She said you can start on Monday."

LeAnna couldn't help the onrushing emotions she felt at this woman's blind trust. Alternately trying to blink back tears and keep her lips from quivering, she said, "Thank you, Lettie. Thank you so much."

The older woman turned her attention to the dish towel in her hand, carefully drying the last glass. "Don't you be thinking a thing of it. I know what it's like to be down on my luck. I might not be the smartest person in the world, but I'm smart enough to recognize a good-hearted person when I see one."

LeAnna watched Lettie fuss with her yellow apron, feeling a smile steal across her face. Lettie Trierweller was a lot smarter than she gave herself credit for. And she wasn't the only one who recognized a good-hearted person when she saw one.

Vince took his foot from the accelerator, allowing the patrol car to coast, allowing himself the opportunity to watch LeAnna Chadwick's smooth-hipped gait. Even from this distance, there was no doubt in his mind it was her. No other woman in Millerton had hair the color of shiny chestnuts. No other woman had the ability to cause his hormones this much commotion by just walking down the sidewalk.

Damn, but that commotion felt good.

The images thoughts of her evoked came as no surprise. After all, he was a man, and she was a beautiful woman. But he'd spent the better part of last night telling himself to forget about her, no matter how beautiful, to forget about the secrets she kept hidden deep in her round brown eyes, no matter how haunting.

For Vince, the past year had been a time of growth, of healing. So many questions had finally been answered, questions concerning his father, and his mother, and his half brother, Conor. That had been the biggest shock of all. The fact that Conor Bradley, who'd been his best friend during the first eighteen years of his life, was also his half brother.

Conor had come back to Millerton a year and a half ago. Four months later, he'd married Bekka. As Conor's brother, Vince became an honorary member of Bekka's boisterous extended family. For the first time in his life he felt as if he truly belonged, and for the first time in his life he was thinking about searching for a soul mate, a woman to share his life, a woman who was open and caring and loving. LeAnna Chadwick was secretive, instead of open. Oh, no, falling for her definitely went against his better judgment.

He pulled up closer to her and drew in a slow, steady breath, slow, steady appreciation sneaking lower in his body. Maybe she wasn't the kind of woman he was looking for, but he couldn't help looking at her just the same.

He lowered the other window, ready to call her name. Before he had the chance, she cast a sweeping glance behind her. The woman had the casual movement down to an art form. Art form or not, she was looking over her shoulder. The realization shot warnings inside his head. *LeAnna Chadwick, what are you afraid of?*

She stopped and turned, the abrupt motion sending her skirt swishing in a half circle before falling into place around her legs. Her grin flashed briefly, dazzling and undisguised. It started his blood heating all over again.

"Oh, Vince, it's you."

"You're looking pleased about something," he called.

"I've had some good news."

"Is your car all fixed?"

The breeze chose that moment to sweep across the quiet street. It played with the pale blue fabric of her shirt and rippled along the folds of her full cotton skirt. LeAnna lifted both hands winsomely to smooth her hair away from her face, and Vince had to remind himself to breathe.

Mother Nature was playing havoc with his better judgment.

"No, I'm afraid my car isn't fixed yet," she said. "I just came from talking to Trudy McDowell. The good news is I have a job at the diner."

Two little girls skipped past them, hand in hand. The smile LeAnna gave them was pure and serene. Vince told himself there was no reason he should feel as if he'd just been kicked in the chest. No reason at all.

"Where are you headed right now?"

"To Lettie's. She's watching Casey for me."

"Need a lift?"

She cast another look down the street, again making Vince wonder what she was looking for, what she was afraid of. With a little nod of her head, she hurried to the curb. "Seems that this police car is my only means of transportation these days."

Her subtle humor did it to him again. Snuck up on him just as surely as if she'd fleetingly brushed her lips across his brow. Like a tender kiss, her little touch of humor left him wanting more. His better judgment told him wanting more wasn't very wise.

With the glow of old-fashioned desire heating his thoughts he said, "The Millerton Police Department, at your service, ma'am."

She tossed her hair behind her shoulders and laughed out loud. "And they say southern manners stop on the other side of the Mason-Dixon line."

As far as Vince was concerned, his better judgment could go straight to hell. He'd noticed LeAnna's southern accent before, and wondered where she'd been when she lost all but its faintest traces. He turned left onto Oak Street, left again on Maple. "Now that you have a job, are you planning to stay in Millerton?"

He pulled his car to the curb in front of his house, just as he had a thousand times before. It only took one glance to know that everything looked exactly as it always had. The grass was green, the house white, the sky blue. Even the sight of Rusty pushing a lawn mower across the back of the lot was nothing new. But there was definitely something different about today. He felt that difference in the rhythm of his heartbeat, in the overwhelming desire to take LeAnna's hand in his and draw her near. He fought that desire, waiting to hear whether she planned to leave town, or had decided to stay.

"Now that I've found a job, I'll be staying for a little while, at least a few weeks. In the meantime, I have to find a room to rent." She opened the passenger door and found her feet, hurriedly making her way to Lettie and Bud's.

I'll be staying for a little while. She wasn't leaving today. But she was still just passing through. Once again Vince's better judgment tried to make a stand, telling him that a few weeks wouldn't change the final outcome, telling him he'd be better off if he didn't become involved with a woman who was just passing through.

"LeAnna?"

She spun around to look at him, her eyes serenely compelling, her lips curved into an unconscious smile. Putting both hands to her face, she said, "I'm sorry, Vince. My grandmother taught me good manners, really she did. Thanks so much for the ride."

"Anytime."

He slid from beneath the steering wheel and stood next to the car. With both forearms resting along the top of his open door, he asked, "You're serious about looking for a place to stay?"

She nodded. "Do you know anyone who has a room to rent?"

"You could stay here."

The last time Vince Macelli so blatantly ignored his better judgment, he'd knocked Conor out with his bare fist. He'd been young then, not much older than the boy mowing the backyard today. Back then, he hadn't known Conor was his half brother. He'd been acting on impulse, striking out at his best friend for the sins of their fathers. Vince knew he was acting on impulse again. He hoped the results wouldn't be anywhere near as disastrous.

From this distance, he doubted that LeAnna could see the actual color of his eyes, but he knew she could feel the intensity of his gaze. He knew, because he could feel the intensity of hers.

Even the firm shake of her head didn't chase that intensity away, but she seemed to be doing everything in her power to keep it out of her voice. "It's nice of you to offer, but I can't take charity. And I can't afford to rent an entire house."

He digested her statement, his gaze sweeping to the back of the lot, where Rusty was swiping his hand across his brow. "It wouldn't be charity. You could pay me in another way."

He glanced back at her in time to see her chin come up at least two notches. She squared her shoulders, and placed her hands on her hips.

He smiled sheepishly. "That didn't come out the way I meant it."

"Oh, really? Exactly what did you mean?"

"I've been thinking about renting this house out, but I haven't gotten around to doing anything about it. I've been paying Rusty Trierweller, Bud and Lettie's grandson, to mow the yard. The boy got into some trouble before he came to live with Bud and Lettie. But he's a good kid. Just needs to keep busy."

LeAnna heard a lawn mower rumbling in the distance, and birds tweeting in the trees overhead. The everyday sounds were soothing. Although it was only May, the late-afternoon sun felt warm on her hair and face. The expression in Vince's eyes warmed her in other ways.

"What does Lettie's grandson have to do with letting *me* stay in this house?"

"You and Casey need a place to live. This house is vacant. Since it's ultimately better for a house to be lived in than unoccupied, you'd be doing me a favor by staying here. There's only one catch."

LeAnna raised her eyebrows.

"I'd want you to let Rusty continue to mow the lawn. He's come a long way, but he needs this job. It gives him a sense of pride, a feeling of accomplishment. Besides, a little sweat never hurt anybody, especially not a fifteen-year-old boy. So, what do you think?"

Vince was walking toward her, and LeAnna didn't know what to say. She'd been prepared to turn his offer down. His honesty had her wavering, leaning toward accepting. She should tell him no. The fact that she didn't had her leaning the other way.

Vince waved to the boy in the backyard. She followed his gaze in time to see the boy raise his hand and wave in return.

The teenager was tall and lanky. From this distance, she couldn't see his facial features clearly, but his hair was strawberry blond. The squareness of his chin was proof that he was on the threshold of manhood. The exuberance in his wave was proof that his regard for Vince was high.

This boy trusted Vince, probably thought the sun rose and set on his shoulders. LeAnna brought her gaze from the teenager, silently weighing her options. She could look for a room to rent, or she could stay here. The choice was hers.

She gave Vince a sidelong glance before saying, "If he mows the yard while I'm living here, I'd want to be the one to pay him."

She finally looked up at Vince, into his eyes, where sunlight illuminated integrity. Wistfulness stole into his expression, stealing into her. With profound clarity, LeAnna realized that before her stood a man with the power to change her life, if she stayed.

Her gaze swept down the column of his neck, down his broad chest, where sunlight glinted off his badge. That badge brought her back to her senses. She couldn't allow him to alter her life. She couldn't allow anyone to.

She was drawn to Vince, but that didn't change the fact that she couldn't stay more than a few weeks. It didn't change the fact that she had a huge responsibility to her child. What she felt for Vince was exciting. It was frightening. It was something she had to guard against. At all costs.

Vince reached into his pocket and brought out a set of keys. He deftly removed three from the round clasp before placing them in her hand. She curled her fingers into a fist around the keys, and slowly pulled her hand from his grasp. As tight as she was squeezing them, she knew the keys would leave an impression in her skin, but she didn't care. Those three keys represented security. They represented four walls and a roof, and three doors with strong locks.

LeAnna knew better than to assume she and Casey would be safe here forever. She couldn't take risks. She especially couldn't take the risk that she'd fall in love with a policeman. She had to call a stop to this immediately.

She took a step back, increasing the distance between her and Vince. Raising her chin, she stared straight into his eyes and said, "Thank you, Officer."

A muscle moved in his jaw, but he didn't speak. She'd called him *Officer*. It had been deliberate. And he knew it.

Taking another backward step, she said, "Guess I'll see you around."

He nodded. "Millerton is a small town."

"Population 5,078, according to the sign at the edge of town."

"As of right now, that's 5,080."

With a firm shake of her head, she said, "Don't have the city change the sign. Lettie's been wonderful, and it's extremely *neighborly* of you to let me stay here. But Casey and I won't be staying forever."

Hurrying across the side yard toward Lettie's, Leanna told herself the ache she felt inside was the need to see Casey, to take him in her arms and assure herself he was safe. Although that was part of it, she knew it wasn't the only reason her eyes burned with unshed tears. This ache had its own place inside her, a place rubbed raw by dreams of forever.

LeAnna braced herself against the pain, against the wistfulness washing over her. As of this moment, she had more than she'd thought she'd have. She'd found a job and a place to stay. For now, that was all she could hope for.

She continued on over the freshly mowed grass, toward Lettie's front door. She didn't look back when the patrol car's door slammed. Her footsteps didn't falter when its engine rumbled to a start. With her hand on the screen door, she heard tires crunch over gravel as Vince pulled out of the driveway.

Casey's chatter carried to her ears. Without looking back, LeAnna took a deep breath, opened Lettie's screen door, and walked inside.

Chapter Three

Vince heard the bell over the diner's front door jingle, but he didn't turn to see who had entered. Instead, his gaze followed LeAnna across the room, watching as she poured coffee and talked to her other customers.

"Jumpin' catfish, Conor," Mac Pearson said, slapping his hand on the tabletop. "I saw Bekka the other day, and I've gotta tell you, she's positively glowing. Didn't take you long to get her in the family way."

Vince met his brother's gaze across the small table. Conor grimaced, and Vince shrugged his shoulders. He took another gulp of Trudy McDowell's strong coffee, and scowled when he burned his tongue.

Conor stared into his own coffee as he said, "Bekka has three months to go. The boys are hoping for a brother, but honestly, Mac, I'll just be glad when it's over."

Mac, who had been like a father to Conor, guffawed. "Bet that isn't what you said six months ago."

"You seem to have forgotten what *you* said six months before that. When you told me I should find a good woman and settle down."

Vince cast a look at the other two men sharing his table. Mac Pearson was in his middle fifties. He had a full head of silver hair and more than his fair share of off-color jokes. He'd been like a father to Conor when Conor needed it most, and he now extended his family to include Vince, as if it were the most natural thing in the world.

Conor was tall and lean and dark. Now that Vince knew they were half brothers, the similarities were obvious. Why hadn't anyone seen it all those years ago?

He and Conor had been best friends as children, both from the wrong side of the tracks, both pretending to be tough. Now that Conor was married to Bekka, Vince saw a change deep in his brother's dark eyes. Conor Bradley had found his life mate, and he'd never been happier.

From the corner of his eye, Vince saw LeAnna disappear into the kitchen. He listened to the ensuing conversation between Conor and Mac with only one ear, letting his gaze roam around the interior of the square room, keeping the kitchen door in his line of vision at all times.

The diner wasn't large, and it certainly wasn't new. There were ten tables and two booths. The tables were full and the booths were empty. People didn't come to the Millerton Diner for privacy. They came to talk. If the place had ever had a color scheme, it wasn't apparent now. The carpet was green, the walls were paneled, the curtains were blue, and the tablecloths were whatever color Trudy felt like using that week. The diner didn't have much in the way of atmosphere. It was the new waitress who provided that.

And the new waitress was avoiding him like the plague.

LeAnna had been working at the diner all week. This was the first time he'd been in. Nothing unusual about that. Vince didn't make a habit of eating Trudy McDowell's cooking. There was nothing unusual about Mac's and Conor's bantering, either. There might be something a little unusual about Vince's perpetual dark mood, but it wasn't unusual for him to keep it to himself.

"Now that I have Conor here married off, I'm gonna see what I can do about you," Mac declared, slapping Vince in the middle of the back so hard coffee nearly spewed in every direction.

Vince swallowed hard, somehow managing to keep from choking. Conor, who rarely pried and almost never offered advice, nodded his head, saying, "Come on, Vince. Mac's right. Maybe you should start looking for the right woman. Someone like Bekka."

Casting his brother a sardonic look, Vince said, "Yeah, well, Bekka's taken, and I . . ."

"Seems like I remember you dating Bekka a few years ago," Mac cut in. "You aren't carrying a torch for your brother's wife, are you boy?"

Conor straightened in his chair. "Just how close were you and my wife?"

Vince held up his hands, warding off more questions. "She wasn't your wife then, Conor. Besides, I dated Bekka before you came back to Millerton. But don't worry. Nothing happened. We never even got close to the serious part. Not enough sparks. Sparks or no sparks, I'm beginning to think Bekka was the last good woman in this town."

Mac, who had warmed to the subject, leaned ahead in his chair. "Maybe there were no sparks because Bekka's not your type. Maybe, instead of a good woman, you should be looking for a woman who sparks your visceral urges, a woman of mystery, a woman who's good at making you feel oh-so-bad."

"More coffee?"

LeAnna's voice shimmered over Vince, drawing his body tight. Mac handed her his cup, handing her a quick line at the same time. She answered him with a knowing smile, a raised brow and a small shake of her head.

She refilled Conor's cup next, and Vince found he couldn't look away. She'd worn her hair up for work, but already curls were pulling free, spiraling at her nape and brow. He wanted to talk to her, ask her how she'd been, but she didn't meet his gaze, not even when she refilled his cup.

"You men care for a Danish this morning?" she asked.

Her voice worked over him like a dream, and Vince found himself saying, "Yeah. Over easy."

Conor cast him a strange look before turning to Le-Anna. "What Vince means is yes, we'd love a Danish. Why don't you bring some over, nice and easy?"

LeAnna nodded, her eyes darting to Vince's, then flickering away again. "Three Danish pastries, coming right up."

She hurried away, and Vince watched her go, noticing the way her hips swayed beneath the pale pink uniform. By the time he brought his gaze back to his coffee, Conor and Mac were both grinning at him.

Mac slapped him on the back again. "Why, you old dog, you..."

"Forget it, Mac."

Mac surged on. "I think I might have wasted my breath on that last little speech about the kind of woman you should search for. Looks to me like there are enough sparks between you and the new waitress to start a forest fire right here on Main Street."

"Looks can be deceiving, Mac," Vince answered.

"Horsefeathers."

This time it was Vince who cast a look at Conor, and Conor who shrugged his shoulders helplessly. Mac Pearson was on a roll. When that happened, there was no stopping him.

"Come on, Vince ol' boy. When she brings your pastry, ask her for a date."

"She doesn't want to see me, Mac. Believe me, she's made that clear."

"How'd she do that?"

Vince practically squirmed beneath Mac's stare. After all, he was a man who kept to himself—his feelings, his thoughts, his emotions. He was a private person, and he didn't appreciate people traipsing through his thought processes. The sooner he steered the conversation to another topic, the better he'd feel. He knew from experience that wasn't going to happen until he answered Mac's question.

Leaning back in his chair, Vince finally said, "She made it pretty clear when she practically hit me over the head with a kitchen chair."

Mac laughed out loud, slapping the tabletop with glee. "Jumpin' catfish! That doesn't necessarily mean she doesn't want to see you. In fact, that could mean she's real interested."

Vince shook his head. "And donkeys fly."

"I mean it, Vince. When she comes back with our breakfasts, find out where she's staying."

"I know where she's staying."

Together, Mac and Conor asked, "You do?"

Vince took turns nodding and shaking his head. They were both so obvious. "She's staying in my old house."

"You sly dog, you," Mac declared with a grin.

"It's not what you're thinking, Mac. Old Alvin Parmeter ran a stop sign last week and hit LeAnna's car. She's only staying until she can pay to get her car fixed, and when she does, she'll be on her way."

"Maybe. Maybe not."

Before Vince could argue, LeAnna brought them their pastries, hurrying away again without meeting his eyes. Watching her go, Vince grumbled, "There's no *maybe* about it, Mac. She's made up her mind. She'll be leaving town soon."

"She could change her mind. It's a woman's prerogative, you know," Mac insisted.

Vince's gaze slid away, straight to LeAnna's. She quickly averted her eyes. After a time, he did, too.

"I don't know, Vince," Mac said, his tone taunting. "I'd say the woman is interested, all right. Real interested. I'd say she's having as much trouble keeping her eyes off you as you are keeping yours off her."

Thankfully, Conor changed the subject. Vince did his best to follow the conversation, but it was a long time before his heart stopped hammering in his chest.

Sitting on the back stoop, her arms wrapped around her knees, LeAnna listened to the sounds of the neighborhood. A screen door banged a few houses away, and every once in a while strains of music from a marching band carried on the gentle breeze.

She squinted against the bright evening sun, its warmth, along with the everyday sounds, making her feel drowsy. Casey jabbered contentedly as he dug in the dirt at the base of the steps, and LeAnna slipped out of her shoes. She'd spent nine hours on her feet at the Millerton Diner, and it felt oh-so-good to relax.

Even though she couldn't see through the hedge, she could hear voices in Lettie's backyard. Casey stopped digging and listened. Jabbering his version of Rusty's name, he looked up at LeAnna, his eyes bright and happy.

"Do you want to go over and say hi to Rusty?" she asked, slipping her shoes back on.

Casey grasped the small, slightly bedraggled teddy bear Rusty had given him and toddled away toward the gap in the hedge. Hurrying after him, LeAnna couldn't help but laugh at the way he screeched with pleasure.

Lettie had watched Casey while LeAnna worked these past four days, and while he liked Lettie and Bud, her little boy *loved* Rusty. No wonder. The teenager allowed Casey to follow him from one end of the house to the other. In fact, LeAnna wasn't sure which boy had more fun together, the toddler or the teen.

"LeAnna," Lettie called, the minute she'd ducked through the gap in the hedge. "Come on over."

Squinting against the evening sun, LeAnna's smile broadened. "Casey heard Rusty's voice," she explained, glancing at her three blue-eyed next-door neighbors. Her breath caught in her throat as she met another pair of eyes, these dark brown.

It was happening again, that curious swooping sensation she felt every time she saw Vince. In a tiny corner of her consciousness she heard Bud, Lettie and Rusty call hellos to Casey, but the rest of her attention was focused on Vince.

What was happening to her? It was all she could do to glance at Lettie and say, "I didn't know you had company."

"Shoot. Vince here ain't company," Bud replied. "He told Rusty he could have this old motorcycle if they can get it running. And we're all just taking a look at it."

Rusty glanced up at LeAnna and quickly averted his gaze. He ran his hand over the exhaust pipe and quietly said, "Isn't she a beauty?"

The *beauty* Rusty referred to was an old black-and-silver Honda that looked as if it had seen better days. It had two flat tires, and a couple of broken spokes. As far as LeAnna could tell, those were its *good* features.

"A real beauty," she agreed, pretending not to notice the slight blush tingeing Rusty's young face. Casey squatted down, mimicking his new friend, and LeAnna laughed out loud.

Her gaze was inexplicably drawn to Vince's once again. Laughter was still on her lips; an answering smile was on his. Somehow, it felt right, it felt good, to be sharing laughter with this man.

"Do you think you can get it running again?" she asked.

He shrugged his shoulders, and for a moment, everything else receded to some other plane, as if she and Vince were alone in the backyard. In that moment, she studied him unhurriedly. His face was full of strength, his eyes, his nose, his beard-roughened chin. Even as she told herself she couldn't afford to have romantic notions about him, her gaze strayed to his mouth. With her heart thudding heavily in her chest, she wondered what it would feel like to kiss him.

The world came back into focus, and she lowered her eyes. Pulling her thoughts together, she told herself she had to get out of there, away from what she saw deep in Vince's eyes, away from whatever it was that drew her to him.

In a voice shakier than she would have liked, she said, "Casey and I have to be going. It's time for his bath."

Vince wasn't surprised when the kid let out a shriek of disapproval at his mother's mention of leaving. After all, the boy was pretty happy where he was, and boys were notorious for disliking their baths. He wasn't surprised that he couldn't take his eyes off LeAnna as she ducked through the hedge with her screaming child in tow, either. But the way she'd looked at him, desire illuminating her eyes, surprised him beyond words.

Just this morning, Mac had said there were enough sparks between him and LeAnna to start a forest fire. At the time, Vince had been afraid the sparks were one-sided. Now he knew that wasn't true. Even though she did her best to ignore it, she felt the pull of attraction as strongly as he did.

Vince answered Rusty's questions about carburetors and gas lines, and listened as Bud and Lettie argued about what to plant in their garden. But his mind wasn't really on motorcycles or gardens. His mind was on LeAnna, more specifically on seeing her again, because, whether she claimed she was just passing through or not, he wanted to see her again.

"Oh, oh, Rusty," Lettie said. "Looks like Casey left that ol' stuffed bear you gave him. You'd better take it on over to him, before he misses it and starts a-hollerin' again."

Vince was careful not to smile as he scooped the tattered teddy bear from the ground. "That's okay, Rusty. I'll take it back on my way home. Help me push this motorcycle into the garage first, will you?"

Together, they put the cycle away. Lettie reminded Rusty to do his homework, and the boy sputtered that he couldn't wait for summer vacation to begin. Bud finally turned to follow Rusty inside, and Vince, with Casey's stuffed bear tucked beneath his arm, ducked through the gap in the hedge.

LeAnna heard the soft rap on the back door. Being careful not to disturb Casey, she deftly rose from the rocker Lettie had loaned her, automatically glancing out the front window. There were no cars parked in the street, and none in the driveway. Staying in the shadows, she peeked at the back door.

An unexpected warmth filtered through her, a warmth that had more to do with the tall, broad-shouldered man silhouetted on the back step than with the higher-than-normal May temperatures. It was the same every time she saw him. Even as she told herself she was mistaken about the way Vince made her feel, even as she told herself she had no intention of permitting herself to become involved with him, she turned the lock and opened the door.

Vince stood on one side of the screen, she on the other. Holding a tattered brown bear in his hand, he whispered, "It looks like Casey fell asleep without this."

She smiled her thank-you as she unlatched the outer door. Vince walked inside and tucked the teddy bear beneath Casey's arm. Her eyes met Vince's, and neither of them moved away. For a moment, she thought he was going to kiss her, right there, with Casey sleeping in her arms.

"It's a nice night," he whispered. "Do you want to sit on the back steps for a while?"

There was really no reason the idea of doing something as common and ordinary as sitting on the back step on a warm May night should fill her with so much yearning. Yet it did.

She'd been here nearly a week, and she'd welcomed the solitude of small-town life. Time had passed quickly while she was at the diner, and she'd cherished every minute of her evenings with Casey. The solitude had a way of turning to loneliness once her baby was asleep, loneliness that no amount of counting could chase away.

"Come on, LeAnna. What do you say? We might see the first lightning bugs of the season."

She heard the underlying sensuality in Vince's voice. Gazing into his eyes, she recognized another emotion, too. He was lonely. As lonely as she.

Choosing her words carefully, she murmured, "I'd like that, Vince." With that, she pressed a kiss to Casey's smooth brow and hurried from the room to carefully tuck him into the makeshift bed on the floor.

Vince was already sitting on the back stoop when she returned. LeAnna slipped through the screen door and lowered to the step next to him, tucking her skirt around her legs.

The sun was out of sight, but its presence still lingered in the pink and orange streaks low in the sky. A car went by, and from somewhere a mother called her children inside.

Softly she said, "You can tell a lot about a neighborhood by listening to its sounds. Earlier I heard horns and drums."

"The high school marching band was practicing for the Memorial Day parade," he answered. "It's the same every year."

Of course. This was the kind of town that had high school bands and Memorial Day parades. This was the kind of town where people knew their neighbors, where people like Lettie left their doors unlocked. It was the kind of town where kids played baseball in the summer, and went ice-skating in the winter. LeAnna thought it would have been a wonderful place to raise Casey.

"What was it like growing up here?" she asked.

Vince met her gaze across the short distance separating them. He was aware of the curiosity in her eyes. She wanted to know what he'd been like as a child. He'd rather show her what he was like as a man. He'd rather take her in his arms and kiss her, and he'd rather not stop there. But she'd already told him she was just passing through, and he didn't want to give her another reason to leave. So, instead of doing what he wanted to do, he began to talk.

"This neighborhood was a lot different when I was growing up. The houses were run-down, the people inside more so. Back then, the voices of children and adults alike were raised in argument more often than in play."

"Even Bud and Lettie's?" she asked softly.

"Even theirs."

"Why?" she asked.

Why? Vince's thoughts returned to his childhood. "Back then, this was considered the wrong side of the tracks. Too many people made too little money and, for one reason or another, had some kind of score to settle. Back then, people were restless and angry."

"And now you're not?"

A hot ache started in his stomach and settled lower. He'd been talking about the neighborhood as a whole, but she'd seen right through him, and asked if *he* was still restless and angry.

Vince had been restless and angry most of his life. He'd blamed it on his childhood, on a father who had hated him, and on the secrets his mother had been forced to keep. Once he knew that LeRoy Macelli hadn't been his real father, he'd tried to put the past behind him. He'd decided to look for an honest woman and settle down. He'd dated several women over the years, women who'd never hinted at leaving Millerton some day. Not one of them had eased the restlessness deep inside him. Not one of them had caused his heart to hammer against his ribs by simply looking into his eyes. Only LeAnna did that.

Leaning closer, he said, "I'm over the anger, but there's only one thing I can think of that would alleviate the restlessness."

Her dark lashes swept down to her cheeks, then back up again. Vince knew she'd heard the huskiness in his voice, and he knew she understood what he wanted. Instead of answering by telling him about her own needs, she lowered her chin and slanted him a sidelong glance, saying, "I thought you wanted to show me lightning bugs, not lightning bolts."

Once again, her tiny hint of humor snuck up on him. It filtered through his thoughts and found its way to his chest. He didn't know how she'd done it, but he suddenly felt like laughing, and that was one thing Vince Macelli didn't do very often.

He saw a smile play along the corners of LeAnna's mouth. And he realized he *liked* this woman. He liked her inner serenity, her sneaky humor, her natural grace. Mostly he liked the way he felt every time he came within twenty feet of her.

Stars were beginning to twinkle into view, and the air was beginning to cool. In a minute, he'd leave, so that LeAnna could go back inside, where it was warm. In a minute, but not yet.

She was still wearing the pink uniform she'd worn at the diner. Her hair might have started the day on top of her head, but now most of it had escaped to curl freely about her neck and forehead.

He'd leave in a minute. First, he wanted to touch her.

He raised his hand slowly, gliding his palm over her shoulder and up to the side of her face. He combed his fingers through her hair, gently tipping her face toward his. Her hair felt soft beneath his fingertips, soft and wavy and slightly cooler than his hand.

Light spilled from the kitchen, bathing one side of her face in a golden glow. Her lashes fluttered down, then back up again, her eyes delving into his even as he drew closer.

He'd leave in a minute. First, he wanted to kiss her.

His mouth touched hers in a feather-light caress. Her lips were soft, and her sigh filled him with a delicious sensation of wanting. He deepened the kiss, lingering, savoring her touch, her scent and her taste. Her lips parted beneath his, and the kiss took on a dreamy intimacy, one that left Vince wanting more. So much more.

Before all his good intentions went up in smoke, he turned his head slightly, breaking the kiss. Fighting the strain of desire, he pulled in a deep breath. "Maybe I'd better show you those lightning bugs *and* lightning bolts another time," he whispered huskily.

They drew apart slowly, their gazes locked. Her eyes were large and luminous. He saw passion, but he saw something else, too. There was integrity and strength and tenderness. And there were also secrets.

She turned her head before he could see anything else. "Do you see lightning bugs often in this yard?"

He'd rather talk about lightning bolts, the passionate kind. He grimaced good-humoredly and said, "Almost every night. There's just something about this yard that draws them." Just as there was something about her that drew him.

"Look," she said, pointing into the backyard. "There's one now."

Vince saw the tiny flash of light near the back of the lot. In a voice slightly laced with passion, he said, "Guess that only leaves those lightning bolts."

LeAnna knew that a smile had broken out across her face. Inside, she was smiling, too. Suddenly, she felt almost lighthearted. For the first time in a long time, she thought it might be possible for her to have a normal life. The very idea filled her with hope and joy.

The air had cooled, yet her skin had warmed from the inside out. Smiling into the night, she whispered, "I've always liked lightning b—"

LeAnna stopped cold. Something moved near the back of the lot, something large and shadowy. For a moment, she froze, her eyes trained on those shadows. There was no sound, other than her blood thundering through her brain, but she'd seen something. She knew she had.

She jerked to her feet, her thoughts whirling at the speed of light. *He found us. Oh, my God, he found us!*

"Leanna, what is it?"

Vince's voice came as if from far away, so far away she barely heard. She tried to form a plan in her mind. She could run inside and grab Casey and run out the front door. But if Nick had found her here, she knew it would only take him minutes to outrun her on foot.

Nick had come close to finding her twice. Once in Kentucky, and again in Pennsylvania. Both times he'd used force to enter her dwelling. Force was the only way Nick knew.

She quickly scanned the backyard. Breathing in through her nose and out through her mouth, she tried to get herself under control. *Think, LeAnna, think.* Her thoughts focused, and a plan began to form. She'd gotten away from him before. She'd do it again. She had to. Casey's life depended on it. So did hers.

A shadow streaked through the gap in the hedge, and LeAnna turned like a cyclone. Strong hands clasped her shoulders, stopping her forward motion.

"It's a dog, LeAnna. It's just a dog."

She strained against Vince's powerful grip only for a moment, only until his words seeped past her fear. *It's a dog, LeAnna. It's just a dog.* With her hand on the door's handle, she turned her head and raised her gaze to his.

His jaw was clenched, and his eyes were narrowed. His whole demeanor was tense, as tense as the silence that grew tight between them. His hands fell away from her shoulders, and LeAnna let out the breath she'd been holding, feeling her body shake from the effort to keep herself erect. Without a word, she opened the door and walked inside.

She stood at the sink, staring out into the dark backyard. The door bounced twice as Vince came inside, but she didn't turn around. She could practically feel his gaze boring into her back, could practically feel his tension and hear the questions zinging through his brain.

"Are you going to tell me what that was all about?"

She finally turned. His eyes were still narrowed, but his hair was mussed as if he'd run his fingers through it. Both his hands were on his hips. It reminded her of the way he'd stood the first time she saw him. He'd been wearing his badge then. He might as well have been wearing it now, because Vince Macelli was a cop, in uniform or out of it.

She stared at him for what seemed like forever. She wanted to tell him why she was so frightened. She might have, if he weren't a policeman.

Taking a step closer, Vince said, "Are you in trouble with the law, LeAnna?"

She felt the hysteria rising in her chest. Fighting against it, she said, "Do you trust me enough to believe what I say?"

He looked at her so hard and so long she felt like a slide under a microscope. But she didn't blink, and she didn't turn away. She just let him look his fill, praying he saw her for what she was. An honorable woman.

She knew the instant he was through. His breath escaped him all in one *swoosh*. He closed his eyes and slid his hands into his pockets. When he opened his eyes again, she finally let out the breath she'd been holding. His eyes held plenty of questions, but no suspicions.

In a voice raspy with emotion, he said, "I don't know how, and I sure as hell don't know why, but yes, LeAnna. I trust you."

It took everything she had not to cry. He trusted her. His belief in her was a gift, but his trust was a treasure, one she'd never forget.

Her relief was so profound Vince wouldn't have been surprised if she slumped against the counter at her back. But she didn't. Instead, she breathed through her mouth, relaxed her shoulders and cast him a tremulous smile, as if his answer meant a great deal to her. He remembered the way she'd pressed a kiss to Casey's forehead a short time ago, and the way she'd nurtured Rusty's enthusiasm over fixing up that old bike. She'd told Rusty the motorcycle was a beauty.

LeAnna was the real beauty.

Before him stood a woman who had suffered in the past. He didn't know how or why. He wanted to ask, but now wasn't the time. Not if he wanted to see her again. Not if he wanted her to grow to trust him. And that was exactly what he wanted.

"In answer to your question," she finally said, "no, I'm not wanted by the law. Everything I've done has been morally right, and absolutely necessary. That's all I can tell you."

The tears he saw brimming in her eyes were nearly his undoing. LeAnna might not have broken the law, but she had a guilty conscience just the same. He should know. He'd grown up with a guilty conscience. He'd pretended to be a tough kid, uncaring that the man he thought was his father didn't love him. He'd acted tough, developed an attitude. Underneath the bravado, underneath the black T-shirts and practiced sneer, had been a bewildered boy, a child with a guilty conscience.

He hadn't been able to name the emotion he'd seen in LeAnna's eyes the first time they met. She'd told him she was just passing through, and at the time he'd thought she was hurrying toward a new destination. Now he realized that wasn't the case. She wasn't running to someone or something. She was running away.

Last year, when he finally learned the truth, when his mother was finally able to tell him that Sam Bradley, Conor's father, had been Vince's father, too, he'd vowed to put the past behind him. He wanted to find an open, caring woman to spend his future with. He hadn't entered into the search for the right woman with many requirements. She didn't have to be a certain height or have hair that was a certain color. But he'd promised himself that the woman he chose wouldn't be harboring secrets. Most of all, the woman he loved wouldn't leave him someday.

So much for self-made promises. He'd found the woman he wanted. She was keeping secrets about her past, and she'd made no bones about the fact that she wouldn't be staying in this town.

"Look, Vince," she murmured. "It's getting late, and I have to be up early in the morning to go to work, so..."

She motioned toward the door, and he clamped his mouth shut on anything he might have said. She'd been afraid of shadows in her backyard. Her fear had been so intense he'd felt it. He didn't want to leave her, but in reality he knew he had no right to stay. He could have demanded that she tell him who she was afraid of, but in her present frame of mind, he had a feeling it would be useless.

He began to walk toward her, his steps sure and even. "All right, LeAnna," he said, his voice deceptively low. "I'll go, for now. But I'll be back."

He came to a stop directly in front of her. "After all," he whispered, "there are still those lightning bolts I promised to show you."

She opened her mouth in surprise a moment before he brushed his lips against hers. Without saying another word, he turned and strode through the door.

He was on the first step when he heard her lock the screen door. He'd barely made it to the bottom when she turned the lock on the back door.

Heading across the back of the lot toward his place, he cast a look all around. Clouds played hide-and-seek with the moon, and a slight breeze stirred the leaves high in the trees. Otherwise, the neighborhood was quiet. A twig snapped under his foot, reminding him of the way LeAnna had snapped to attention only minutes ago. Her fear had been real. As real as her passion.

Within minutes, he'd reached his own back door. Turning the knob, he strode inside and flipped on a light. He hadn't even bothered to lock up before he went on over to Bud and Lettie's earlier. LeAnna bolted her doors at all times.

What are you afraid of, LeAnna? And why won't you tell me?

Chapter Four

LeAnna called a goodbye to Lettie and Casey. Still smiling, she hurried along her neighbor's narrow sidewalk. There was no sense denying that there was more spring in her step this morning. There was no sense denying why. Vince Macelli trusted her.

Bud waved as he pulled from his driveway in his old green truck. She returned his wave without missing a step and glanced all around her. Eleven children were waiting for the bus down on the corner. LeAnna counted them twice, because she could have sworn it would take twice that many to make so much noise. Her steps slowed as she watched a shiny black Mustang turn the corner. When it pulled up to the curb out front, she came to a complete halt.

Vince.

She'd wandered from one end of the house to the other after he left last night. Counting floor tiles and light bulbs, she'd silently listed all the reasons she should steer clear of becoming involved with him. All those reasons flew right out of her mind every time she relived his kiss, every time she remembered his words: *I trust you.*

He'd been right there when she fled into a panic at the first sign of movement in the backyard. He knew she'd been terrified of something. *She* knew he wanted to understand why. But he hadn't demanded answers. Instead, he'd looked into her eyes and given her his blind trust.

He was looking at her much the same way right now. He wasn't wearing his uniform, and his left arm was resting along the lower edge of his open window. His head was tilted upward slightly. As always, there was a hint of arrogance in the cut of his jaw, and innate intelligence and independence everyplace else.

"Can I give you a lift?" he asked.

"Do you mean it?" she asked.

He quirked one eyebrow and said, "I always mean what I say, LeAnna."

For reasons she didn't understand, she believed him. Vince Macelli was a complex man, one who wasn't always easy to read. Although she had no intention of confiding in him, she suddenly felt like grinning. "In that case," she said, "I'll take you up on your offer."

Vince would have liked to say something provocative in return. After all, he could think of several other *offers* he'd like to make, every one of them a lot more stimulating than driving her to work.

She strode around the front of his car with an economy of movement that amazed him. But her speed didn't fool him. He knew she'd taken in every detail of his car, and wondered if she'd compliment him on his '67 Mustang. Every other woman he'd ever known had. Some of the comments had been trite. *I just love a man with a fast car.* Others had been out and out come-ons. *You can tell a lot about a man's car by looking under his hood.* Or *I'll bet you like your cars fast and your women the same way.* Every trite little come-on had ground him the wrong way. After all, he hadn't hauled this car from the junk heap and fixed it up to impress women. He'd done it because this was the car he wanted. Plain and simple.

He knew LeAnna noticed his car's shiny black exterior and refurbished interior, just as he knew she was aware of every other car in sight. She cast a practiced eye at the bucket seats, at the knob-topped shift lever on the floor and the Mustang emblem on the dash. Finally she glanced at the street behind them. "Is everything all right?" she asked, as if she were wondering why he hadn't pulled away from the curb.

That was it. No trite line, no hollow compliment. Just a straightforward question, murmured in a voice that filled him with warmth. Vince cast her a sidelong glance and tipped his head toward the door. "Everything's fine. I just wouldn't want to have to arrest you for failing to wear your seat belt, that's all."

This wasn't the first time they'd bantered about that particular Michigan law. She'd asked him about it when he gave her a ride to his old place, the first time they met. Like that other time, her head tipped to one side and her eyelashes came up. It was a wry look of amusement he was coming to know.

"Do the police in Michigan really spend their time arresting people for that?" she asked.

"It all depends," he replied.

"On what?"

She clicked her seat belt into place, and he finally pulled out into the street. With both hands on the wheel, he said, "I suppose it would depend upon extenuating circumstances. They have a way of changing the law's outlook, you know."

Vince knew what he was doing. He was trying to tell her that the law wasn't cut-and-dried, and neither was he. He was trying to tell her she could trust him.

He'd lain awake long into the night, thinking about her. It had been so easy to imagine her in his old bed, staring out his old window, gazing at the same stars he was gazing at. It had been so easy to remember the look deep in her eyes when he'd told her he trusted her. The difficult part hadn't been believing in her. The difficulty had been staying in his own bed, when all he wanted to do was run back through the neighborhood, straight to her locked back door.

There was only one reason he hadn't. He didn't want to scare her away.

He took his eyes from the street for only an instant, and found her watching him intently. "Are you telling me you've been known to look the other way where the law is concerned?" she asked.

"I don't look the other way, LeAnna. But I have been known to try to help. And I'd like to help you."

After a long moment, she asked, "What if there was nothing you could do?"

"I guess you'll just have to trust me on that one," he answered.

There. He'd tossed the word *trust* out between them, like a Frisbee on the beach. Now the issue was in her hands, and it was up to her to decide what to do with it.

LeAnna stared wordlessly at Vince, her heart pounding an erratic rhythm. All these rhetorical questions were making her dizzy. Or was Vince doing that? She'd been surprised last night when he told her he trusted her. Surprised, and downright shaken. More than anything, though, she'd been touched. She'd gone to sleep thinking of him, and woken up this morning with his name on her lips.

As she prepared herself and Casey for their day, she'd thought about the way Vince had kissed her. She thought about the tenderness in his fingertips, and in his eyes. Lettie had told her that Vince had been on the receiving end of his father's abuse. LeAnna found herself wanting him to be on the receiving end of her gentleness.

She knew she wouldn't be staying here forever. She also knew it was the little things that made life worthwhile. Friendship was one of those things. When she left Millerton, she'd like it if she and Vince parted as friends. Special friends.

Up ahead, the light on Main Street turned red. Vince downshifted, the car's engine rumbling with leashed power. She cast a look up the street, where Ned Thelen was lowering the awning in front of his hardware store. Two other men were stringing a banner between two lampposts, high above the street.

"It looks like they're decorating for the Memorial Day parade," she said.

He took his eyes off the red light and said, "Since half the population of Millerton goes up north for the long weekend, they always have the parade the Friday before. That's tonight. Were you thinking of going?"

She turned her head to look at him. "I might."

"I'm driving the mayor through the procession. You could ride along."

Shaking her head slowly, she said, "I'm afraid I'm not much for the limelight."

A horn blared behind them. LeAnna glanced back, trying not to grin when Vince pressed his foot to the pedal and ground the lever into first, finally reacting to the green light. He gunned around a corner and pulled into the alley behind the diner.

"Conor's sister-in-law is having a party after the parade," he said. "Would you and Casey like to go with me?"

"How big of a party?"

"Not huge," he answered. "Conor and his wife, Bekka, and their kids will be there. Bekka's sister, Mara, and her husband are having the party, and the rest of their family are always invited, along with Bud and Lettie and Trudy, and a few others."

LeAnna hadn't done much socializing these past six months. She'd never been much of a partier, but a quiet small-town party sounded nice.

"There will be lots of food, and other kids for Casey to play with. What do you say? Want me to pick you up around seven?"

She placed her hand on the door handle and considered her answer. "The party sounds like fun, and I'd like to go. But I think I should meet you there."

Although she wasn't looking at him, she heard his sharp intake of breath as he asked, "Why?"

Her gaze flickered over the trash cans lining the back alley as she said, "I don't want anyone to get the wrong idea about you and me."

She pushed on the door and slid to her feet, clicking the door shut behind her. Peering through the open window, she said, "Thanks for the ride, Vince. I'll see you tonight."

"I haven't even told you where the party is being held." He ground out the words between his teeth. "How do I know you won't end up at the wrong house?"

Her gaze slid to his, and her lips eased into an unhurried smile. "I guess you'll just have to trust me on this one."

Vince's breath caught in his chest as he watched her turn and stroll toward the diner's back door. Morning sunlight glinted off the curls high on her head like a halo. He knew darn well the woman was no angel.

He felt as if every dormant emotion he'd ever had were coming to life. It felt good and bad at the same time. He'd wondered what she'd do with the trust he'd thrown her way. She'd casually tossed it back to him. It had hit him right between the eyes. She had a way of surprising him, of staying one step ahead of him. She stimulated him, and he liked it.

On impulse, he jerked on the door handle and quickly jumped to his feet. "LeAnna?" he called over the roof of his car.

She turned in the doorway.

"Just for the record, what do you think of my car?"

She brushed an errant curl away from her cheek, her brown eyes slowly roaming from one end of the car to the other. Her gaze met his, and in an oddly gentle voice, she said, "I think it suits you."

The door swung shut behind her, and she was gone.

For a moment, Vince just stood there, his mouth gaping open, his eyes trained on the place she'd been. Somehow, laughter found its way into his chest, pulling him from his trance. He slapped his hand against the top of his car with uncharacteristic glee before sliding back into the driver's seat.

After a time, he shifted into reverse and slowly pulled out into the street. Her words played through his mind like a hot summer breeze, bringing him incredible pleasure, but not much relief.

She thought his car suited him? He thought she suited him, too.

LeAnna strolled across the grass, slowly taking in all the commotion. This was the small party Vince had referred to? There were thirty people in the backyard alone. She recognized some of the faces as customers from the diner. Several of the guests were laughing, others were eating from paper plates. Children darted between tables and adults, screeching with happiness as they played.

"Bud-dy," Casey proclaimed, pointing his little finger toward a man standing in the shade of a tall sycamore tree.

Slowly LeAnna made her way toward Bud and Lettie, systematically categorizing every person she saw. By the time she reached her neighbors, she was breathing a little easier. Not one person here looked the least bit threatening.

Unless she counted Vince.

There was no denying that Vince Macelli was a good man, and she'd have to be a fool to believe he'd ever threaten her physical well-being. But she'd have to be an even bigger fool not to realize that the feelings he evoked deep inside her had the power to change her. They frightened her, and invigorated her, and drew her.

He was standing with a small group of men, a dozen feet from Bud. There was an inherent strength in the set of his shoulders, a touch of stubbornness in the way he folded his arms at his chest. Several of the other men wore shorts. Not Vince. It was easier to imagine him in nothing than in something as casual as shorts. Her thoughts clouded with the potent image of Vince wearing nothing. She bent down to set Casey on his feet, hoping her hair covered the blush rising to her cheeks.

From his position several feet away, Vince saw LeAnna blush. The fact that she tried to hide it from him made him pretty sure thoughts of him had caused it. The very idea sent a ripple of desire through him.

Mac and Conor didn't seem to mind that he only half listened to their conversation, but every once in a while their gazes followed his, straight to LeAnna. The only reason he hadn't gone directly to her the moment she arrived was that she'd told him she didn't want anyone to get the wrong idea about them. Vince didn't give a rip what anyone else thought about him and Leanna. But he cared what she thought. So, instead of planting himself at her side, he watched her from afar.

She stayed in the shade with Bud and Lettie, and Vince wondered if she could be unaware that every man within a hundred yards of her had noticed her presence. She was wearing a blue skirt and blouse he'd seen before. The outfit wasn't fancy, and it wasn't expensive, but then, it wasn't her clothes that made LeAnna beautiful.

"I'd say it's time to make your move with the new waitress," Mac told him. "After all, you've waited just about long enough to keep from lookin' too anxious."

Mac slapped him on the back, and Conor looked at Vince curiously. Vince answered them both with a shrug. Without a word, he stepped around the other two men and strode toward the one woman who'd occupied his thoughts all day long.

LeAnna saw Vince approaching, and was relieved when Bud snagged his attention a few paces away from her. While the men talked about the weather, she noticed Casey toddling toward her, the fingers of one chubby little hand closed into a tight fist.

"What do you have in your hand?" she asked with a smile, all sorts of possibilities flitting to mind.

Casey opened his fingers slowly. "Bug," he said.

Gently taking his hand in hers, she murmured, "That's a ladybug."

Sensing freedom, the tiny orange insect took off like a rocket. LeAnna laughed out loud at Casey's surprised expression. "Yadybug fly, Mommy," he said.

She scooped him into her arms and kissed his smooth cheek. "Ladybug fly," she repeated, feeling breathless with wonder. Casey's growing vocabulary never ceased to amaze her, but nothing filled her with more joy than when he said, "Mommy."

Casey pointed to the glass of red liquid in Lettie's hand. Without a moment's hesitation, the older woman strode away toward the punch bowl. Still smiling, LeAnna said to

Bud, "While Lettie's getting his punch, I think I'll take Casey inside and wash his hands."

Vince strode closer. He hunkered down a little, bringing his face even with Casey's. "Have you been playing in the dirt again, slugger?" he asked.

"Dirt," Casey answered solemnly.

LeAnna's gaze locked with Vince's. In that moment, everything seemed right with the world. Casey was overcoming his shyness and fear, and Vince was looking at *her* as if he saw something special in her eyes.

"Come on," he said quietly. "I'll show you where the bathroom is, so you can clean him up."

Vince and LeAnna both turned toward the house, slowly stepping out of the shade. He led her inside and watched as she scrubbed Casey's pudgy hands. They talked about inconsequential things, but below the surface they communicated something else entirely.

She'd responded to his kiss last night. Now she responded to him on an even a deeper level. Both affected him like glory, puffing his chest, pulling at his lips and heating his thoughts. Vince wasn't sure what he felt for LeAnna. But he was sure he wanted her—in his bed, yes, but in other ways, too.

Sidestepping a group of blond-haired children, he tried to get hold of his heated thoughts. Behind them, Bud said, "Ned Thelen just told me he heard we're supposed to have a thunderstorm later on tonight."

Vince watched LeAnna glance up at the sky, where clouds were gathering, far in the east. He remembered the previous night, when he'd told her he'd like to show her lightning bugs and lightning bolts. The look she slanted his way now told him she remembered, too. His thoughts heated, along with his body, sending the blood rushing through him with a roaring din.

A commotion broke out in the backyard. Voices rose in panic. Vince and LeAnna both turned toward the sound.

"Somebody help! She can't breathe!"

LeAnna straightened and swung around so fast her head spun. Several people were gathered around the picnic table, where a young woman was apparently in trouble.

"Slap her on the back!" someone yelled.

"Tip her upside down!" someone else cut in.

LeAnna sprang into action. She plucked Casey from her hip and thrust him into Vince's arms. Seconds later she pushed through the crowd around the picnic table, her gaze trained on the woman gasping for air.

Within seconds, the woman's face went from red to white. She was choking. She needed oxygen. And she needed it now.

LeAnna dived between two of the guests. "What's her name?" she shouted.

"Mara," someone answered.

"Mara, stand up. I'm going to help you," LeAnna promised. She slid both her arms around the other woman's waist and pulled her to her feet.

Voices rose all around them. LeAnna barely heard. She stood at Mara's back and placed her hands at strategic positions directly below Mara's rib cage. With speed and purpose, LeAnna squeezed, thrusting her fist into Mara's midsection.

She felt Mara's breath *whoosh* out of her like air bursting from a balloon. With that breath, the item that had been lodged in her throat flew across the table. Mara took a gasping breath, coughed, and took another.

She staggered, and Vince was suddenly there, lowering her to the bench with one arm, easily holding Casey in the other. LeAnna went down to her knees and automatically took Mara's wrist in her hand. With her eyes trained on her watch, she counted the beat of the other woman's pulse.

LULLABY AND GOODNIGHT 69

Everyone was talking at once. A little girl was crying. A woman was pushing a glass of punch into Mara's hands.

"She can take a sip in a minute," LeAnna said, in a soft, reassuring voice. "What she needs most right now is air."

LeAnna did a careful inspection of Mara, recognizing her as the person who had welcomed her to the party when she and Casey first arrived. The young woman's color had improved, and she was breathing regularly. "I think you're going to be okay," LeAnna whispered.

Mara swiped her fingertips over her tear-streaked cheeks and, in an awe-filled voice, said, "You saved my life."

A cheer went through the crowd, and LeAnna finally became aware of all the people who had gathered. Vince and Casey and Bud and Lettie were there. So was Trudy, along with several others she didn't recognize.

Taking a deep breath, LeAnna said, "Don't think a thing of it. I just used the Heimlich maneuver. It comes in pretty handy in my line of work."

Being careful not to jostle the child in his arms, Vince took a small step back. Someone said they were going to rest easier now that they knew their new waitress wouldn't let them choke on Trudy's cooking. People laughed. Everyone began talking at once, and in the aftermath of the excitement, no one seemed to remember the way LeAnna had sprung into action, or the way she'd automatically taken Mara's pulse.

Vince doubted *he'd* ever forget.

LeAnna had said the Heimlich maneuver came in pretty handy in her line of work. Everyone else might believe she'd meant as a waitress. After all, a waitress could have learned the lifesaving procedure. But it wasn't likely that a waitress would automatically take a person's pulse.

Somewhere, sometime, LeAnna Chadwick had had medical training. So what was she doing working at the diner? Why hadn't she tried to get a job at the small local hospital? What was she hiding?

Word had reached the front yard, where Mike Miller, Mara's husband had been talking to another group of friends. He made his way through the crowd, hurrying to his wife's side. "Mara!" he called. "Are you okay?"

Mara made light of the situation, obviously uncomfortable with all the attention. "You always told me I'd end up eating my words, Mike. Well, that time, I almost choked on them."

The guests laughed again, and slowly dispersed. LeAnna moved to do the same, but Mara caught her hand. "It's LeAnna, right?" Mara asked.

LeAnna smiled in answer. Mara surged on. "You saved my life, and I haven't even said thank-you."

"You're welcome," LeAnna whispered, taking another step back.

"Wait," Mara insisted. "You're new in town, aren't you?" At LeAnna's nod, she continued. "Where are you staying?"

LeAnna's gaze unerringly found its way to Vince's, and it was all she could do to swallow the lump in her throat. Casey looked utterly content in this strong man's arms, but she nearly floundered beneath Vince's intense look. He'd noticed the way she reacted to the serious situation, and was trying to understand.

Mike Miller's voice cut into her thoughts. "If you ever want another moment's peace," he told her teasingly, "don't tell my wife where you live."

She forced herself to laugh, the action helping release the knot that had formed in the pit of her stomach. She exchanged a few words with Mike and Mara before finally turning her attention back to Vince.

Casey was still perched on Vince's left arm. Although Vince held him stiffly, Casey didn't seem to mind. Her child gazed up into Vince's eyes with so much trust that tears swam in LeAnna's eyes. Six months ago, after she lifted Casey from his crib and fled, he'd whimpered at his own shadow. She knew she'd saved his life that night, and she couldn't stop the tear that ran down her cheek at the memory of Casey, dirty and hungry and too weak and terrified to cry.

There was barely any trace of that child now. And no matter what it had cost her, LeAnna would have done it all over again.

She strode toward Casey and Vince, the movement drawing both their gazes. Her breath caught in her throat at how right Casey looked in Vince's arms. Anyone who didn't know better could easily think they were father and son. But LeAnna knew better. Casey's father had never made him feel secure.

Pushing those thoughts away, she smiled at Casey and asked, "Are you having fun?"

"Fun!" he repeated, evidently in no hurry to leave the security of this strong man's arms.

She finally met Vince's gaze. He seemed to be the only one who had noticed anything amiss about a waitress who'd instantly reacted to a life-threatening situation. Good heavens, she'd told him she didn't want anyone to get the wrong idea about them, and had thrust Casey into his arms as if it were the most natural thing in the world, as if he'd held her child a hundred times before. Strangely enough, Casey didn't seem to mind. Neither did Vince.

LeAnna wasn't accustomed to using people, and she didn't like it. Now she owed Vince an explanation. But how much could she tell him?

Tipping her head to one side, she finally said, "Thank you for watching Casey for me. Is your arm getting tired?"

He hiked the child a little higher on his arm and said, "He's heavier than he looks."

His wry grin made LeAnna laugh. "He's a strong little boy."

Vince's voice dipped lower as he said, "Then he takes after you."

There was really no reason for tears to gather in her eyes, no reason for LeAnna to feel as if she'd just been paid a precious compliment. She held out her hands to Casey. "Come on, sweetheart. Let's go home."

Casey grinned with total innocence and blithely leaned toward her, trusting her completely to catch him. She settled him on her hip, looking up just in time to see Vince flex his arm.

"Can you tell Vince bye-bye?" she asked Casey.

Casey opened and closed his fingers a few times in his version of a wave. Vince looked at him with amusement, and simply said, "Bye, slugger."

LeAnna turned to go, feeling a certain sadness that her time with Vince was drawing to an end. She'd only taken a few steps before she swung around again. Vince hadn't moved. He was standing with his hands on his hips, a serious expression on his face, his gaze on her. Screwing up her courage, she said, "If you want to stop by later, we could watch for lightning bugs again. And maybe talk."

She sensed a flickering heat deep in his eyes, and felt an answering heat steal into hers. It would have been easy to get lost in the way he looked at her, but LeAnna couldn't lose her way. On some deeper level, she sensed that Vince understood. He finally smiled, and she felt their friendship blossoming.

"Go ahead and start walking," he said, his features deceptively composed. "I'll wait a few minutes, then pick you up." After an intentional pause, he said, "After all, we wouldn't want anyone to get the wrong idea about us."

It was her turn to be caught off guard, her turn to smile wanly long after he strode away. He was a complex man, all right. And he drew complex responses from her. He radiated a vitality that drew her, that made her feel as if she were drifting on a cloud.

"Whuzat?"

"That," LeAnna said, following the direction of Casey's finger, "is a very special man." To herself, she added, "And I'd better be careful, or I'm never going to want to leave."

Vince ducked through the gap in the hedge, wondering if he'd given LeAnna enough time to get Casey settled in. The child had wanted nothing to do with bedtime as long as he was there. It had been almost comical to watch the boy's stubbornness thwart all LeAnna's attempts to coax him to sleep. With the excuse that he needed a walk, Vince had headed on over to Bud and Lettie's. The last thing he said to LeAnna had been "I'll be back."

He took the steps two at a time and effortlessly pulled on the screen door's handle. The fact that it didn't budge stopped him in his tracks. LeAnna locked her doors at all times, even when she knew he was coming back.

Thunder rumbled as he rapped softly on the old wood. She opened the inner door as the first sprinkles began to fall. LeAnna unlocked the screen door, and he strode inside, straight to the counter. With his back to her, he heard the lock click into place.

Thunder shook the ground, rattling the kitchen window. "Looks like we won't be able to see those lightning bugs tonight," she said.

Slowly turning around, he asked, "Was that really the reason you invited me over?"

She shook her head, the movement sending soft curls dancing around her face. She'd changed her clothes. Instead of a skirt and blouse, she now wore faded blue jeans and a T-shirt that had probably been a bright pink a hundred washings ago. All those launderings might have faded its color, but they'd also softened the fabric so that it draped over her shoulders and delineated the curve of her breasts.

With incredible effort, he brought his gaze to her eyes. She took a deep breath, but it was several seconds before she said, "I invited you here because I feel that I owe you an explanation."

Vince settled his hips more comfortably against the cabinet at his back. With one hand on the counter beside him and the other in his pocket, he said, "I've never been much for obligatory explanations, LeAnna, so let's get one thing straight. You don't *owe* me anything. But if you offered me a beer and some friendly conversation, I might just take you up on it."

LeAnna felt his words drain the stiffness from her jaw and shoulders. She tipped her head to one side, eyeing the lanky man standing in the kitchen. There was nothing unusual about his clothing. Jeans were jeans, and navy shirts were navy shirts. Why, then, did she react completely differently to this man from the way she did to any other?

"I'm afraid I don't have any beer. But if you don't mind instant iced tea, I could offer you some of that."

With a casual shrug, he said, "My mother always drinks iced tea."

LeAnna set about preparing their beverage. She reached into the cupboard for the mismatched glasses Lettie had loaned her, and into the freezer for the ice. "What's your mother like?"

"She's a good woman, about so tall," he told her teasingly, holding his hand at shoulder level. "She looks younger than her actual age, despite living through eighteen extremely hard years. Her hair used to be blond, but now is threaded with gray."

Handing him his glass, she said, "You must have gotten your looks from your father."

"You could say that. Although the man who raised me— and I use the term loosely—wasn't my father. As it turns out, my real father was even worse."

LeAnna motioned toward the table, silently offering him a chair. Evidently Vince was comfortable where he was, because he took a long sip of tea, but he didn't follow her across the narrow room. She lowered herself onto one of the kitchen chairs and pulled both knees up, grasping her hands around her ankles.

"I barely remember my father," she said softly. "He and my mother both died when I was small."

"Did you have any other family?" he asked.

"Luckily for my sister and I, our grandmother took us in. You would have liked my grandma," she said with a smile. "She could cuss out of one side of her mouth and pray out of the other. She raised us poor but proud. Sometimes I think I can still hear her voice echoing across the mountain."

Vince took a long swallow of tea, the liquid cooling a trail from his lips all the way down to his stomach. Funny, it didn't cool his thoughts. It didn't keep his gaze from straying to the front of LeAnna's T-shirt, to the curve of her hips, to the length of her legs.

"How old were you when you left home?" he asked.

Tipping her head to one side, she sighed. "Seventeen. I left right after high school. I went back often over the years, but things had changed. And it didn't feel like home anymore, you know?"

Vince knew what she meant, all right. He glanced around the kitchen, taking in the clean floor, the odds-and-ends dishes, and the bouquet of lilacs filling an old jelly jar. He could see into the living room, where a tattered magazine and a ragged child's book littered one sofa cushion. He'd lived in this house most of his life, and although his mother had tried, it had never felt like home. LeAnna had been here little more than one week, yet her homey touches were everywhere.

He'd heard the homesickness in her voice when she mentioned her grandmother and sister. He felt a similar emotion in his soul right now. Homesickness, loneliness, restlessness. They were all just different names for the same feeling.

He'd come here tonight hoping for some answers to his questions about LeAnna's past. Suddenly, it didn't matter where she used to live, or how she'd come by her medical training. All that mattered was that she made him feel alive, almost young, and until that moment he'd always sworn he'd been born old. The one thing that really mattered was that she was here now. And so was he.

The room had grown quiet, so quiet he wondered if she could hear his thoughts. The iced tea in his hand would never quench this particular thirst. There was only one thing that would do that. One thing. With one woman.

Without taking his eyes off her, he lowered his glass to the counter. The glass teetered. Before Vince could right it, it toppled over, the remaining tea and ice spilling onto the counter.

LeAnna was suddenly there. With fast, efficient movements, she reached for a towel and quickly stopped the stream of tea headed for the edge of the counter. He watched the towel darken as it absorbed the spilled tea, and wondered if his eyes were darkening as he absorbed LeAnna's closeness.

He covered her hand with his, and her gaze slowly climbed to his. They stood close, little more than a foot between them, close enough for him to see the dark rings around her irises, close enough for him to see the glimmer deep in her brown eyes, the glimmer that spoke of kindred spirits.

He glided his hand over hers, over the delicate bones in her wrist, past her slender elbow and the gentle curve of her shoulder. His other hand found its way to her back, bringing her closer. She swayed toward him like a willow, her chin lifting toward his. Her eyelashes dropped down partway, tickling his beard-roughened cheek. Her lips parted on a sigh, and Vince could wait no longer.

Chapter Five

LeAnna closed her eyes and drew nearer. Her mouth met Vince's, the touch of his lips a heady sensation. Last night's kiss had been like a whisper. This was more like a song, warm and vibrant and so in tune with her wants and desires she went weak in the knees. She'd been kissed before, but she'd never been kissed like this, as if the joining of her mouth with Vince's were more necessary than breathing, as if the parting of her lips beneath his were predestined.

His lips were both urgent and exploratory. He moved them across hers, nipping the corner of her mouth, then swooping to capture her lips once again. His tongue probed sensually, and the music deep inside her changed, becoming more primitive, more in tune with her inner voice, more in time with the rhythm of her beating heart. It left her dazed, and yearning for more.

Drawing apart, they both gasped for air. She pressed a kiss to his cheek, to his jaw and his chin. His hand came up to her face, as if he couldn't wait another moment to reclaim her mouth. He gave new meaning to the word *desire*, bringing new sensations every place he touched. She slid her hands around his back, and he moved, fitting her body closer to his. His strong legs straddled hers, his hips rocking slightly against her. The muscles in his back moved beneath her palms as the desire between them intensified.

LeAnna felt weak and strong at the same time, pliant and warm, yet not warm enough. Vince's breathing had deepened, his kisses becoming more soul-reaching. His hands glided across her back, bringing her hard against him, then skimming away again, over her shoulders, down to her waist, and finally to her breast.

His fingers kneaded and caressed, and she gasped, letting her head fall back. Rays of light shone through her closed eyelids as he trailed kisses along her jaw and massaged her flesh. Within moments, the rays of light in her vision changed, shimmying lower. If it had been the Fourth of July, LeAnna might have understood the explosive heat inside her. Since they were only celebrating Memorial Day, these particular fireworks must be coming from Vince.

Through half-opened eyes, she watched his expression as she let her hands trail down his back, down past his hips, kneading his flesh, memorizing his body. He breathed between parted lips, a deep-throated moan escaping on his sigh.

"I want you, LeAnna. Right here. Right now. In every way."

His hands continued to work magic over her body, bringing her such incredible pleasure her thoughts spun. In the middle of it all, she thought about the way he'd looked at her at the party, after she took Mara Miller's pulse. She thought about Casey, and about the guilt she felt over the way Nick had treated him. "You don't even know me, Vince. Not really."

He whispered a kiss along her jaw, and another against her ear. "I know everything I need to know. I know you must have good reasons for keeping your secrets. I know the law doesn't want you. But I do."

His words stilled her movements, but not her thoughts. "How do you know the law doesn't want me?"

He stopped kissing her, and stared deep into her eyes. "Because I asked the computer system a few questions. It didn't give me any more answers than you have."

LeAnna wasn't surprised he'd checked her out. Any good cop would do the same. The fact that her name wasn't on the computer meant there were no warrants out for her arrest. Her mind raced ahead with that information. That meant Nick still hadn't gone to the police, which in turn meant that he still intended to handle this his way.

She had no doubt that Nick would go to the police if all else failed. Evidently he didn't believe that was necessary. He was still out there. Somewhere. And he was still looking for her. God help her, and God help Casey, if he ever found them.

"LeAnna."

She raised her gaze to Vince's face. His eyes were half-closed. She could see the strain of desire in the lines in his cheeks, could hear it in the rasp of his voice as he said, "I want you. And you want me."

Of course he was right, but thoughts of Nick hammered away at her, obscuring her passion. Nick was out there. She had to remember that, and remembering anything wasn't easy when Vince was kissing her, touching her.

"I can't do this," she whispered.

"Why?" he asked, smoothing an errant curl away from her eyes. "LeAnna, what are you afraid of? Are you running from an abusive husband?"

She closed her eyes and shook her head. "I've never been married."

He evidently misinterpreted her choked silence as a sign of a guilty conscience, because he said, "You think I care if you and Casey's father weren't married? My mother never married my real father, and believe me, it was a blessing."

He spread his fingers wide across her breast, and there was no stopping her low groan of pleasure. He smiled with so much tenderness, tears swam in her eyes. She'd ached for that kind of tenderness all her life, and she ached now, because she knew she couldn't reach out and take what he was offering.

"Vince," she said, straightening. "We can't do this."

Vince fought against the urge to wrap his arms around her and prove her wrong, to kiss her and touch her and caress her until she didn't have a coherent thought in her head, until one thing, and one thing only, filled her mind. Her desire for him.

But she was straightening, trying to disentangle her arms, trying to step out of his embrace. She had her reasons for stopping, and it wasn't conceit that made him think they didn't have anything to do with *him*. She'd made no excuses for wanting him. And she made none for stopping, either.

Her passion had been so real, so intense, the air surrounding them had nearly vibrated with it. That had changed when he mentioned checking the computer system for information about her. He might have understood if she'd reacted to the knowledge with anger. The expression in her eyes had changed, but not to fury or rage or even offense. Her eyes had narrowed as if she were calculating time against need.

LeAnna was a little over five foot six. That was on the tall side for most women around here. But her slender build made her seem delicate. The narrow bones in her shoulders felt as fragile as dandelion fluff. He felt the pull of her muscles as she stepped back, and realized her fragility was an illusion. He let her go, wondering where she'd acquired her strength, both physical and emotional.

She turned her back on him, slowly striding to the table where she'd left her iced tea. Her spine was ramrod-straight, and her shoulders were squared. Even so, the deep breath she took caused her whole body to quiver. That involuntary movement made Vince wonder if she was really as strong as he thought.

He drew in his own deep breath, trying to get his thoughts and his emotions under control. Desire was still pumping through his body, making reasoning difficult. He knew a little more about LeAnna now than he had yesterday. Tomorrow he'd learn a little more. For now, he took another shuddering breath and slid his hands into his pockets. "I should be going," he said to her back.

"That would be best."

Vince didn't agree, not in the least, but he was lousy at relationships, and he didn't want to mess up whatever chances he had of having one with LeAnna. Even with the strain of desire lessening, he knew that was what he wanted. A connection, an alliance, maybe even a future, with this secretive woman.

He finally pulled his hands from his pockets and moved toward the back door. Lightning streaked the sky, and thunder rattled the windowpane. With his hand on the doorknob, he glanced back at LeAnna, and found her watching him. He made a quick appraisal of her features, of her dark, curly hair, her smooth-as-satin skin and kiss-swollen lips.

Thunder cracked, and the lights flickered off, then on again. Gazing into LeAnna's eyes, Vince knew they would have experienced their own electrical storm if she hadn't had her own reasons for stopping. The current was there. But the time wasn't right.

"Soon," he said, in a desire-laden voice he hardly recognized as his own.

Without another word, he turned the lock, pulled the door open and darted out into the dark night. His shoes splashed through puddles. The pouring rain kept him from hearing her slide the bolt back into place, but he had no doubt that she had.

By the time he'd made it the twenty-five feet to the driveway, he was soaked through. He hurried to his car, closing himself in and the rain out. He started the engine, then sat peering through the deluge of water. It wasn't difficult to make out the lit windows in his old house. He saw no movement inside, and fleetingly wondered if LeAnna was watching him from the shadows.

With a flick of his wrist, he turned on the windshield wipers and finally backed from the driveway, his thoughts moving in a similar back-and-forth direction. LeAnna was afraid of someone. Vince had no idea who. She was nothing like the kind of woman he'd decided to look for, yet she was the only woman he wanted. She wanted him, too. And if he had anything to say about it, she was going to have him.

Sitting on the front stoop, LeAnna slid out of her shoes and hugged her knees up close to her body. Rusty was mowing the lawn out back. Afraid to let Casey play nearby, lest the machine fling a stone his way, she'd brought him out front. He jabbered as he scooped a plastic measuring cup into a bucket, diligently watering the sidewalk.

Last night's thunderstorm had been short-lived, dumping half an inch of rain, then moving on to the south. Bud had claimed they needed the rain, and Lettie was sure the grass had grown three inches in one day. Evidently Rusty thought so too, because he'd gotten the mower out right after supper.

Through half-opened eyes, LeAnna watched as a gray van slowly turned the corner down the street. Moments later, it glided to a stop in her driveway. A young woman stepped out, bright evening sunlight glinting off her blond hair.

Karlie.

LeAnna rose to her feet slowly. For a long moment, she felt as if she were floating.

The woman stepped into the shade, and LeAnna came back down to earth. Even though she had Karlie's coloring and build, it wasn't Karlie. It was the woman named Mara, from the party last night.

Of course it wasn't Karlie. Karlie was gone. LeAnna knew it, but for a moment she'd hoped it wasn't so. Swallowing, she tramped down the sob that had risen to her throat, and concentrated on what Mara Miller was saying.

Casey scrambled up the steps, clinging to LeAnna's leg. Mara took his reticence in stride, effortlessly bending down closer to the small boy. "Well, hello," she murmured. "Aren't you a sweetheart? It's obvious where you got your dark eyes and curly hair. You look just like your mommy, do you know that?"

Mara's friendly smile slowly put both Casey and LeAnna at ease. LeAnna doubted Casey understood everything Mara said, but he understood the gentle caring in her voice, and he gradually loosened his hold on LeAnna's leg. Mara straightened, and LeAnna found herself smiling into friendly blue eyes.

"I know what you're thinking," Mara insisted. "You're thinking I look a lot better now that my face isn't blue."

LeAnna laughed out loud, and Casey looked up, as if surprised by the sound. With humbling clarity, she realized what these past six months had cost them both. She'd intended to give Casey as normal a life as possible. She'd somehow forgotten that a normal life included laughter.

"My two-and-a-half-year-old son is a little on the shy side, too," Mara said. "If only his twin sisters had a fraction of his reserve. Those two little girls are only six, and could already talk the stripes off a tiger."

LeAnna found herself smiling, thinking Mara's daughters obviously came by their outgoing personalities naturally. She slid her feet into her shoes and swung Casey into her arms.

"Listen to me rambling on," Mara said. "Here I am talking your ear off, and I haven't even told you why I stopped by." Barely pausing long enough to catch her breath, she surged on. "After you left last night, I talked to Lettie. She told me about the car accident you and your baby were in, and how it left you stranded here without most of your things. She said your baby sleeps on the floor, and you never complain. I couldn't stop thinking about the way you saved the day yesterday, and I'd like to at least try to return the favor."

LeAnna looked directly into Mara's eyes and said, "That isn't necessary, Mara. I didn't do anything anyone else there couldn't have done, and..."

"Maybe," Mara said, interrupting her. "Maybe someone else could have helped me, but you're the one who did. Besides, Marc's outgrown his crib, and it seems silly to store it up in the attic when your baby could be using it, don't you think?"

Rusty rounded the front of the house with the lawn mower, and LeAnna never had an opportunity to answer. Mara motioned for him to turn off the motor, and before LeAnna knew how it happened, she'd put the teenager to work carting items from the back of her van.

In the week LeAnna had known him, Rusty had been slightly reserved. Casey adored him, but she'd respected his silence, allowing him to interact in his own way and in his own time. Not Mara. She issued orders and talked a blue streak, seeming not to notice that Rusty answered only in partial sentences.

Weighted down with a large cardboard box containing baby clothes Mara's son had outgrown, LeAnna met Rusty at the door. He was on his way back to his house for the tools Mara had sent him to find so that he could assemble the crib. They both raised their eyebrows as Mara prattled on in the background, and LeAnna's smile broadened as he met her amused expression with one of his own.

Half an hour later, he ducked out the front door again, his relief to be escaping Mara's orders evident in his sheepish expression. Watching him go, Mara murmured, "If he can stay out of trouble, that boy's going to be quite a man someday."

Through the screen door, LeAnna watched Rusty saunter away. "I have a feeling he's going to be quite a man either way," she murmured.

"Whuzat?" Casey asked, pointing into a box on the floor.

"That," Mara answered, "is a toy truck. For you."

Casey squatted down, again asking, "Whuzat?"

LeAnna helped him pull another toy from the box. Laughing, she said, "A lot of children's first words are *mommy* or *daddy*. Casey's was *whuzat*."

"Marc's was *zipper*," Mara sputtered. "Wouldn't the psychiatrists have a field day with that one?" Without preamble, she plopped down on the floor near the box of toys, as if it were the most natural thing in the world. She talked about her sister, Bekka, and her brothers, Todd and Dustin, about her children, Marc, Missy and Mindy, and so many other people Leanna knew she'd never be able to keep them all straight.

Mara Miller spoke fast and laughed often, and LeAnna had a feeling she'd make a wonderful friend. But she'd learned her lesson five months ago, when a woman she thought she could trust had tried to contact Nick. LeAnna knew she and Mara couldn't be lifelong friends. That didn't mean they couldn't be friends while she and Casey were here. The very idea filled LeAnna with an incredible sense of well-being.

"Now that you know all about my family, tell me, what you do think of Vince?"

LeAnna nearly gasped in surprise at the sudden change in topic. Mara surged on, laughing as she said, "I saw you talking to him at my party last night, and when Lettie told me you were staying here, I got to thinking."

LeAnna finally found her voice. "Well, don't *think* another thing of it. Millerton is a nice town, but Casey and I aren't going to be staying here."

"You're sure?"

LeAnna nodded.

Mara sighed. "That's too bad. I was hoping…" Her voice trailed away as she cast an unhurried glance all around. "Vince has kept this house in good condition all these years. But I'm glad you're here, LeAnna, because I think it needs a woman's touch."

Sparkling blue eyes delved into LeAnna's. Mara hadn't said, *His house isn't the only thing,* but she might as well have, because it was there in her eyes, and in her beguiling smile.

LeAnna let her gaze roam around the sparsely furnished room, thinking about Vince's kisses, about what he said and what he didn't say. She was a woman who counted floor tiles and doorknobs, yet she couldn't count how many times she'd told herself she was mistaken about what she saw in his eyes. He was a policeman—a good one, according to Lettie and Trudy. LeAnna doubted he saw himself that way. She wished there was some way to show him what she saw.

"Oh, my gosh!" Mara declared, jumping to her feet so fast Casey looked up from his toy. "It's almost eight o'clock, and I promised Mike and the kids I'd bring ice cream home.''

Within seconds, Mara hurried out the front door. Standing in the doorway, LeAnna watched her go, thinking she knew how it felt to be taken by storm. In fact, she wouldn't be at all surprised if the term had been invented for Mara Miller. The woman was amazing. She talked a mile a minute, and when it came to issuing orders, she rivaled a seasoned drill sergeant. She loved to meddle, but didn't seem to mind when her questions produced no real answers.

LeAnna hadn't stopped to think when she heard voices raised in panic at the party last night. At the time, it hadn't mattered who was in trouble, only that someone was. Now she was glad it was Mara she'd helped. She was glad she'd made a new friend. After all, true friendship was precious.

''See you soon!'' Mara called from her minivan's open window. With a honk and a wave, she backed from the driveway and was gone.

See you soon. The casual phrase echoed through LeAnna's mind as she prepared Casey for bed. Vince had said something similar when he left last night. Only there had been nothing casual about the way his voice faded on that one word.

Soon.

Even now, she wasn't entirely sure what he'd meant. He'd see her soon? They'd kiss again soon? Or soon they'd make love?

Each of those possibilities filled her with a greater sense of anticipation than the last. Each, in turn, was more difficult to get out of her mind.

Thoughts of all three stayed with her long after she'd put Casey to bed, long after she'd poked through the boxes of clothes Mara had loaned her, long after she'd taken a long, hot bath and climbed into bed. Long after she'd run her hand across the letter from her sister, then lovingly tucked it back under the mattress, where it was safe.

She tried to think of something else, but thoughts of seeing Vince, of kissing him, of making love with him, had moved into her subconscious, and it seemed as if they were going to stay. Shortly before midnight, she reached her hand toward the window, gently lifting the gauzy curtain aside. Long before she was through counting the stars in the sky, drowsiness washed over her. Even as she lounged on the edge of sleep, thoughts of Vince whispered through her mind.

Vince Macelli always means what he says. She hazily remembered him saying so. He'd tell her what he'd meant. *Soon.* LeAnna's eyes fluttered closed. And she slept.

"Whuzat?"

"Those are church bells," LeAnna answered, fastening the buttons on Casey's adorable little outfit.

"Look at you!" she declared, taking both his hands in hers. "You are so dapper!"

Casey looked down at his "new" clothes, practically bending in two in order to see himself. He straightened, and with an impish grin he clapped his hands in glee before setting off across the living room like a dandy little rooster strutting his new feathers.

LeAnna laughed at his antics, feelings swelling her heart. She could have attributed the lump that rose to her throat to the church bells nostalgically chiming in the distance. But she knew it wasn't nostalgia that made her feel like laughing and crying at the same time. It was a kind of happiness that hurt around the edges, because it was so sweet, and so fleeting.

Casey poked through his newfound toys, and LeAnna ran her hand down the stack of clothes Mara had loaned her. The pile wasn't large, but it contained an airy aqua-colored skirt and a matching scoop-necked top, two pairs of shorts and five shirts, even a white cotton nightgown with tiny tucks along the bodice. Mara had insisted the clothes were from her prechildren days, when she'd been twelve pounds thinner. Secondhand or not, every item was lovely.

A tiny splash of color caught LeAnna's eye. She reached into the bottom of the box and pulled out a bright pink bikini. She felt her mouth drop open at the way it fit in the palm of her hand. Just the thought of wearing it intensified the desire she'd felt in Vince's arms Friday night, the desire she'd taken with her to bed last night and woken up with this morning.

"Bye-bye, Mommy?" Casey asked, drawing her from her thoughts.

"Do you want to go bye-bye?" she asked, smoothing a wrinkle from the shirt she'd decided to wear.

He nodded with his entire body, and LeAnna wondered where they could go. It was Sunday. Bud, Lettie and Rusty had gone to church, and the diner was closed. "I know," she said, an idea popping into her head. "Do you want to go for a walk?"

Without a word, he toddled toward the door.

"Wait a minute, Casey. I'm not ready."

"Now," he insisted.

Laughing, she said, "Soon."

Her laughter trailed away with that one word. She stepped into peach-colored shorts and finished fastening the row of tiny buttons down the front of the shirt. The clothes smelled faintly of the lavender pomander she'd found tucked inside the box. It was a feminine scent, and LeAnna was already painfully aware of the feminine sensations whispering through her.

"Go bye-bye. Soon," Casey said at her knees.

LeAnna gazed at her reflection. "All right, sweetheart, we'll go bye-bye. Soon." Even in the wavy mirror, that one tiny word sat on her lips like a kiss.

Vince glided his hands across the newly painted wagon, pleased with its transformation. He'd found the old West-ern-Flyer along the road while on duty a few weeks ago. Since somebody had decided to use the back road for a gar-bage dump, he'd stashed the rusty old wagon in the trunk. At the time, he'd planned to fix it up for his two nephews. But he hadn't been thinking about Jimmy and Jason when he started working on it yesterday, or when he applied the final coat of paint last night. He'd been thinking of Casey Chadwick. And LeAnna.

He squirted a little oil on the squeaky wheel, then stood back to view his handiwork. He was all finished, and the wagon looked almost as good as new.

Brushing his hands on his jeans, he glanced around. The sun was already high in the sky, but the neighborhood was still quiet. It was always like this on Sundays. Later on, people would venture out into their backyards. Children would play, and adults would sit on their decks and talk. Somebody would barbecue chicken, and everyone else would wish they'd thought of that.

All Vince could think about was seeing LeAnna again. Two days ago, he'd touched her intimately. And his body still ached with the desire to touch her again.

After he left her Friday night, he'd had every intention of seeing her again. Soon, real soon. Although the need to talk to her, to touch her, had been strong, he'd realized he couldn't go charging into her yard like a bull hot on the scent of a female. Although, God knew, that was about the way he felt.

LeAnna had gone up like dry tinder at his touch. And yet she'd stopped. Vince knew darn well she had good reasons for doing so, just as she had good reasons for insisting she was just passing through Millerton. He wondered about his chances of convincing her to stay.

He pulled the wagon out of the garage and lowered the overhead door. He caught a movement from the corner of his eye, a flash of peach and white and baby blue. Evidently people were venturing outside a little earlier than usual.

He picked the wagon up and started for his old place. Anticipation lengthened his stride, deepened his breathing and chased through his bloodstream. Halfway down his driveway, the splashes of color came into focus. His steps slowed, then stopped entirely.

Casey was squatted down on the sidewalk in front of the house next door. Vince smiled as he heard the child's inquisitive *whuzat*. If he strained his ears, he could make out the barely-there southern cadence of LeAnna's patient reply. Anticipation continued to course through him, but slower, heavier. There was desire, yes. There was always desire at first sight of LeAnna. But watching her with her child, he also felt a growing sense of awe. With renewed patience, he lowered the wagon to the ground. And waited.

LeAnna noticed a movement out of the corner of her eye and automatically searched for its source. Vince. His hands were on his hips, and his feet were a comfortable distance apart. There was a bright red wagon near his knees, and a contemplative glint in his eyes.

"I was on my way over to your place," he said, in a voice velvet-edged, yet strong.

He stayed where he was in his driveway, and LeAnna and Casey slowly walked closer. Motioning to the wagon, he said, "Someone used a country road for a trash dump. Since your car is in the shop, I thought a new set of wheels might come in handy."

Casey scampered to the wagon, immediately trying to climb inside. "Looks like he likes it," Vince said quietly.

LeAnna lifted Casey into the wagon before saying, "He's in his glory today. Last night Mara Miller brought over some toys and clothes her son can no longer use. She even loaned me a crib, although Casey wasn't too sure about sleeping in it last night."

"You mean he liked sleeping on the floor better?" Vince asked.

Smoothing a lock of Casey's hair from his forehead, she grinned and said, "I'm afraid he likes to be held while he falls asleep."

"Smart kid."

At a loss for something to say, she stared wordlessly at Vince for what seemed like a very long time. Attraction pulsed between them, and she couldn't help thinking about holding him, and being held by him in return.

He was the one to break the silence. "So," he said, his voice slightly raspy. "Mara's taken you under her wing."

"You could say that," she replied.

"Good old Mara," he grumbled. "My brother married her sister about a year ago. Mara's been trying to marry me off ever since."

LeAnna compared the warmth she'd seen in her new friend's eyes to the traces of irritation she heard in Vince's voice. Mara was the type of woman who cared deeply for her family. If she was playing matchmaker for Vince, it was only because she wanted him to be happy.

"I have a feeling Mara means well," LeAnna said. "In many ways, you're lucky to have such a warm extended family."

"In many ways," he agreed. "What about you? Do you have any family anywhere?"

She felt her throat thicken at the merest mention of her family. She hadn't talked about this in a long time, not only because there had been no one to tell, but because the pain was still too new.

Casey, never one to sit still for long, climbed out of the wagon. He toddled over to the edge of the driveway, where he contented himself with a pile of stones. Keeping him in her line of vision, she turned her gaze to Vince.

"When Mara first pulled into my driveway last night, the sun played tricks with my vision, and I thought she was my sister." LeAnna paused, remembering. "Then I realized it couldn't be my sister, because Karlie died last year. But for that split second, I wanted to believe it was true so bad it hurt."

Vince heard the echo of pain in LeAnna's voice, and sensed that she wanted to talk about this. "Was your sister anything like you?"

That brought a smile to her lips. Shaking her head, she said, "Not in looks. Karlie was two years younger than me. She was blond and petite and, for the most part, docile. Except when it came to leaving the mountain, that is. We never had much money, and I knew that if we ever wanted to make a life for ourselves, we'd have to do it off the mountain. Karlie refused to go with me. I went back as often as I could, but she wouldn't even consider leaving."

A thousand questions circled through Vince's mind. This was the first time LeAnna had been willing to talk about her past. He wanted to know everything about her, but was afraid she'd close up if he pushed for answers. Instead of rattling off several questions, he carefully decided on a few. "Where did you go? After you left the mountain, I mean."

"To California."

Vince had wondered where she'd been when she lost all but a lingering trace of her southern accent. Now he knew. "Is that where you met Casey's father?" he asked.

"No," she said, her voice seeming to come from far away. "I met him back on the mountain."

Before Vince's eyes, the clouds cleared from LeAnna's face, as if she'd realized what she'd said, or what she'd been about to say. Her chin came up, but not before he caught a glimpse of sorrow, and surprise. And fear.

So, Vince thought to himself, he'd been right about the fact that LeAnna was running from someone. He didn't know why she was running, but at least now he knew who she was running from. She was afraid of Casey's father, and she undoubtedly had good reason.

"Of course you miss your sister," he said quietly. "But, LeAnna? You're not completely alone."

She turned her head away from him, her gaze trained on her child. "You're right," she murmured. "I have Casey."

That wasn't what he meant, but he refrained from saying so.

LeAnna felt weepy. She'd always miss her sister, would always wish things had been different, but until that moment, she hadn't realized how much she'd missed talking about her. Vince Macelli was an incredible man. If circumstances were different, she would have told him so.

Her gaze strayed behind him, where late-morning sunshine glittered off a high-pitched roof. "So this is your new house," she said quietly.

The L-shaped home was constructed of brown brick. Sunlight glistened off its windows. Lush green grass was growing all around them, and a new walk curved toward the front door. This house was definitely more modern than his other one. She saw an old apple tree way out back, but there were still no shrubs, bushes or flowers. She remembered when Mara had said that Vince's old house needed a woman's touch. LeAnna thought his new one did, too.

Thoughts of Mara brought LeAnna from her musings. "Mara's really been trying to marry you off?" she asked.

At his nod, she continued. "You might not appreciate her interference, but she has a good heart, Vince. The next time she tries to match you up with someone, maybe you should give it a try.''

Vince didn't shrug his shoulders in an offhand way, as she'd expected. Instead, he stood statue-still, his hands on his hips, his eyes squinting against the sun.

From the beginning, she'd sensed an aloofness about him, a seclusion that set him apart. There was a place deep inside him, a place where loneliness echoed like dripping water in an ancient dungeon. Maybe she was the only one who saw it, heard it. Maybe that was because she felt it, too.

She pulled her gaze from his dark eyes, letting it trail down the strong column of his throat, over his shoulders, all the way down to the newly painted red wagon at his knees. Casey toddled over. Pebbles clanked and pinged to the bottom of the wagon, and Casey clapped his hands at his own cleverness. She smiled in spite of the tears stinging her eyes.

Loneliness didn't change anything. Not Vince's, or hers. It didn't change the fact that she couldn't allow herself to get too close to this man. If she did, she'd never want to leave. And she *had* to leave.

Casey was growing strong and healthy. If she stayed, and if Nick found them, her life, and Casey's, could very well come to an end.

She couldn't stay. She'd known it all along, and she'd be wise to remember it from now on.

"Casey!" she called, trying for a light tone of voice. "Are you ready to finish our walk?"

Casey jabbered his answer, already toddling toward her. LeAnna said a hasty goodbye to Vince and, taking Casey's hand, turned to go.

"Don't forget his wagon."

Vince's quiet voice drew her around. Eyeing the wagon and the man, she said, "I think it would be better if you gave it to your nephews."

His gaze didn't waver as he said, "I fixed it up for Casey. It's his." He tipped it over, easily emptying it of the stones and pebbles.

LeAnna sighed heavily, feeling a sensation of inevitability wash over her. Casey was thrilled with his new wagon. As she helped him climb up, his excitement was almost catching. Fixing the wagon for Casey had been a nice gesture. Although she appreciated it, she had to be careful that Vince didn't get the wrong idea. She had to make sure he knew that she and Casey weren't staying.

"I'm sure Casey's going to enjoy riding in this wagon. It was kind of you to offer to give it to him, Vince, but we can't keep it, at least not forever. It won't fit in my car when we leave."

She reached for the handle. With a word of caution to Casey to hold on, she slowly pulled him down the driveway. Vince stared after them, uncertain whether to cuss up a blue streak, or follow them. In the end, he did neither. He stayed where he was in the driveway until they were no longer in sight.

He heard voices coming from the next yard. Just as he'd thought, people were beginning to drift outside. Someone had started a grill, and the smell of barbecued chicken wafted on the breeze, just as it did every other summery Sunday in Millerton.

There was one huge difference this particular Sunday. Today he felt like slamming his fist into a brick wall. And he hadn't felt like doing that in years.

He thought about the way her eyes had glazed over as she talked about her sister, and some of his anger evaporated. He thought about the way she'd raised her chin when she told him she couldn't keep the wagon because she and Casey couldn't stay, and a few things became crystal-clear.

There was no denying the desire still pumping through him, but no matter how mad she made him or how much he *wanted* her, the fact remained that her plans didn't include him. She had her reasons, and his instincts told him those reasons had to do with Casey's father. Since she didn't trust *him* enough to confide in him, gut instinct was all Vince had. And his gut instincts told him LeAnna Chadwick was one woman who could break his heart.

How many times had she told him she was just passing through? Five, six? Hell, he didn't need to be hit over the head. She wanted him to leave her alone. Vince decided then and there it would be better for everybody to give the lady what she wanted. After all, he knew firsthand how it felt to be left behind by the people he cared about. His real father had left him before he was even born. Emotionally, his other father had left early in his childhood. Even Conor, who'd been his best friend, had left when they were both on the brink of their eighteenth birthdays. Conor had come back, but he'd been gone twelve years. Vince didn't want to miss LeAnna for that long.

He stuck his hands in his pockets and slowly walked inside.

Chapter Six

LeAnna clipped Casey's tiny red shorts to the makeshift clothesline, then moved on to his small striped shirt. Her pink waitress uniform came next, then her blue cotton skirt.

Lettie had offered the use of her old washer and dryer, but LeAnna had declined. She preferred to remain self-sufficient in as many ways as possible. Besides, she enjoyed doing her and Casey's laundry by hand. The rhythmic movements were soothing, and she took comfort in seeing the colorful row of clothes and towels gently waving in the breeze.

It was the beginning of June. She'd been in Millerton nearly two weeks. Although her life here was as temporary as the clothesline strung between a tree and the white-washed garage near the back of the property, it was also as anchored as each sturdy clothespin.

Casey was thriving on the relative normalcy of his days. It had been two months since he'd had a nightmare, even longer since he'd been frightened of his own shadow. Le-Anna went to work each morning, and pulled Casey around the block in his wagon every evening. Rusty had begun ambling over after supper each night, and Mara and her children had stopped by twice.

It was the kind of life depicted in Norman Rockwell paintings, the kind of life LeAnna would have loved to hold on to. If the realization that she couldn't stay sometimes made her feel sad, she didn't allow herself to indulge in self-pity.

She knew she was going to miss her new friends when she left. She missed Vince already.

In the four days since he'd *loaned* Casey the wagon he'd come into the diner only once. He'd been cordial, and although a warm expression she'd come to recognize had stolen across his face, he hadn't mentioned seeing her again. She'd bumped into him this morning over at Bud and Lettie's. Again his gaze had rested on her, but he'd made no move to draw her into conversation.

She finished hanging up the last item in the basket, calling herself a fool for wondering how he was. She'd as good as told him she had no wish to become involved with him. And he was respecting her wishes. It was the best—for both of them. Though sometimes the best didn't feel very good.

She stayed close to Casey, answering at least a hundred *whuzat?* questions before taking him inside for his nightly bath. After he'd splashed and played in the bathtub for half an hour, she dried him off gently and dressed him in a clean diaper and lightweight pajamas. He fell asleep in her arms in Lettie's old rocker. All LeAnna could think about was the time Vince had insinuated that *he'd* like to be held as he fell asleep, too.

She laid Casey in his bed, then wandered out into the living room, where she put her hands to her cheeks and slowly turned around. Mara hadn't known how LeAnna could possibly live with no television or radio. Normally, it wasn't a sacrifice. She'd never much enjoyed sitcoms, and the news was usually all bad. But tonight, as she roamed through the sparsely furnished rooms, she wouldn't have minded turning on a radio or television. At least the house wouldn't be so utterly quiet.

LeAnna opened the back door and aimlessly wandered outside. From the top step, she gazed all around her. It was dusk, that hazy time between day and night when the sky is a smoky shade of gray, when the sun is down but the moon isn't out, when the breeze dies away and even the tiniest sounds hang in the air.

Dusk used to be her favorite time of the day. She found little pleasure in it tonight, for tonight she couldn't escape the feeling that she'd lost something precious, something she hadn't even known she had. Shaking her hair away from her face, she took the box she used as a makeshift clothes basket and strode to the clothesline.

The high-pitched squeal of a car's brakes split the quiet evening. She heard a hollow thud, and a tormented *yip*. Seconds later, a car's engine faded in the distance.

"LeAnna! LeAnna, come quick!" Rusty's voice cracked on the last word.

LeAnna dropped the clothes into the box, her feet already moving toward the front of the house. Rounding the tall hedge, she saw Rusty hovering over a black dog as if he weren't sure what to do. She ran closer, and they both went down on their knees along the edge of the street.

"There, there," she crooned to the injured animal, trying to gauge the extent of the dog's injuries and whether or not it was friendly.

Cautiously she allowed the dog to sniff the back of her hand. Satisfied that he wasn't hostile, LeAnna asked, "Do you know whose dog he is?"

Rusty shook his head. "Never seen him before."

"He's skinny enough to be a stray," LeAnna said, glancing up when a car slowly curved around them.

"What are we going to do?" the boy asked.

LeAnna heard the tremor in Rusty's voice, and saw the spark of some indefinable emotion in his eyes. Trying for a soothing tone, she said, "The first thing we have to do is get him out of the street. Can you help me pick him up?"

Sweat broke out on Rusty's upper lip as he slid one hand beneath the dog's back legs. When the animal whined in pain, he jerked his hand away, going noticeably pale. "He's hurt real bad, LeAnna," he said. "He's going to need a vet."

Keeping her voice soothing, LeAnna said, "I don't have a car, Rusty. Are your grandparents home?"

"Grandma is, but she doesn't drive. I know," he said, jumping to his feet. "I'll get Vince."

Rusty started to run before he uttered the last word, his long strides taking him out of her sight before she could do more than blink. By the time the black Mustang drove up, a few minutes later, Lettie had joined LeAnna in the street, and dusk was steadily turning into darkness.

Lettie hurried back inside to call the local veterinarian's emergency number. Still on her knees at the dog's side, LeAnna heard two car doors slam. Without looking up, she knew Vince was there.

He lowered to his knees near the dog's back. "Is he seriously hurt?"

The way the animal lay there, too frightened and in too much pain to move, made answering difficult. The animal's helplessness reminded her of Casey, that night a little over six months ago. Raising her gaze to Vince's, she shrugged. He stared into her eyes, and it was so easy to get lost in the way he looked at her.

She drank in the sight of him. His hair was damp, and she inhaled his freshly-showered scent. In the gathering darkness, his eyes appeared as powerfully compelling as he was.

Lettie hurried toward them, wringing her hands. "Doc Masey says he'll meet you at his office in ten minutes."

Rusty bent to pick up the dog, who once again yelped in pain. "I think his back leg is broken," LeAnna said softly. "Vince, it would be better if you picked him up from your side. Just be careful you don't jostle that leg any more than necessary. We don't want him to go into shock."

Vince slid his hands beneath the dog, cautiously rising to his feet. With the animal in his arms, he and Rusty turned toward the car. LeAnna and Lettie stayed where they were on the edge of the street, watching. Rusty and Vince both looked back at LeAnna, but it was Rusty who said, "Aren't you coming?"

"Casey's sleeping," she said softly.

"If Rusty would feel better if you went along," Lettie said quietly, "go ahead. I'll go on over to your house and sit with Casey until you get back."

LeAnna glanced from Rusty to the house to Lettie, all in the span of one heartbeat. "All right, Lettie," she said. "But keep the doors locked, okay?"

The gray-haired woman narrowed her eyes and said, "If that's what you want, I'll lock the doors. Now go on."

Again LeAnna thought the older woman was smarter than she gave herself credit for. Doing as Lettie instructed, LeAnna hurried to the car where Vince and Rusty were waiting. She opened the passenger door for Vince, who carefully placed the injured dog on the front seat.

Everyone climbed inside, and within minutes they'd reached the veterinarian's clinic. Doc Masey pulled up right behind them. By the time the vet had the door unlocked, Vince, with the dog in his arms, and Rusty and Leanna were all lined up single file behind him.

Doc Masey asked a few questions. Oddly, it was Rusty who answered. The doctor took the injured animal and disappeared on the other side of another door. Vince, Rusty and LeAnna all took a seat in the small waiting area. Within minutes, Vince stood and began pacing. LeAnna and Rusty glanced up, exchanging a look. Waiting was not Vince Macelli's long suit.

Ten minutes later, the balding doctor returned. "You don't have any idea who the dog belongs to?" he asked.

Rusty shook his head, and LeAnna answered, "I think it's the same dog I saw in my backyard one night last week."

She remembered everything about that night in vivid detail. She remembered Mara's party, and Vince's kiss. She remembered the touch of his fingertips in her hair. And she remembered her panic when she'd thought that stray dog was— As if of its own volition, her gaze turned to Vince's. The expression in his eyes told her he remembered, too.

Doc Masey's gravelly voice drew her attention. "The dog is malnourished, and he isn't wearing a collar or tags. His back leg is broken. The X ray shows this isn't the first time. There are scars under his coat, and since he's a stray, the most humane thing to do would be to put him to sleep."

"No!" Rusty jumped to his feet.

"I know it sounds cruel, son," Doc Masey explained. "But he wouldn't feel a thing, and—"

Rusty cut in, his chest heaving from his labored breathing. "That other broken bone, and those scars. You think he's been beaten, don't you?"

The old doctor nodded gravely.

"Set the leg," LeAnna said softly.

The vet looked at her warily as he said, "Most people don't want to spend a lot of money on a stray."

"I'll pay," three voices said in unison.

The doctor looked at the three of them with raised eyebrows before nodding and striding from the room. LeAnna, Vince and Rusty all glanced at each other, then slowly looked down. Suddenly it seemed there was nothing to say.

Rusty and LeAnna took their seats, and Vince strode back to the corner on the other side of the room.

Rusty leaned ahead in his chair. He rested his elbows on his thighs, fidgeting with his clasped hands. "Seems like there ought to be a law against a person beating an animal. Humans, too, for that matter."

A hot ache grew in LeAnna's throat at her young friend's anguished tone. "There are laws," she answered quietly. "It's just that some people don't obey them."

Rusty glanced sideways at her. "I'll bet that dog ran away first chance he got. He'd rather be hungry than beaten. He's smart, all right. Sometimes a person's gotta be smart to survive, huh, LeAnna?"

The ache in LeAnna's throat turned into a huge lump. Tears swam in her eyes, and she found herself thinking that Rusty's grandmother wasn't the only astute Trierweller.

Across the room, Vince ran his hand over his hair, unobtrusively watching the exchange between Rusty and LeAnna. Before his eyes, a bond was forming between them, and Vince was almost jealous.

That woman had a way with people, a way with strays. He'd seen her innate gentleness with Casey, and with that injured dog, too. Now he was witnessing it with Rusty. He knew darn well she'd bestowed kindness on *him,* too, and fleetingly wondered how long it had been since anyone had given that tenderness back to her. There was something about this woman, something unique and quiet and warm. He'd love to return her tenderness, and slowly turn it into passion. Vince felt his body tighten, just thinking about it.

Rusty and LeAnna continued to talk on their side of the room. Vince continued to think on his.

LeAnna wasn't going to stay in Millerton. She'd told him several times. Four days ago, he'd finally listened, and since he didn't relish the idea of her taking a piece of his heart with her when she left, he'd decided to stay away from her. These past four days had been the longest in his life.

The door opened, and Doc Masey walked through, his arms filled with one large, groggy, straggly black mutt. "Normally, I'd want to keep a dog overnight. Since he's a stray, and I'm sure you'll want to keep costs down, you can take him on home. Just keep a dish of fresh water nearby, and by morning he'll be wanting food. Bring him back in two weeks, so I can take another look at him."

Vince nodded as he handed the doctor some money, then took the dog from his arms. Rusty said, "I'll pay you back, Vince. I mean it."

Gently running his hand over the dog's head, the boy said, "Come on, Chief, let's go home."

LeAnna smiled and said, "My grandma always says a pet named is a pet claimed. Rusty, I'd say it looks as if you have yourself a dog."

Vince felt his eyes narrow. LeAnna glanced up at him, and he wondered if she realized what she'd just said. Rusty opened the door for him, and LeAnna ran ahead to help him put *Chief* in his car. Vince followed, his mind racing. He distinctly remembered asking LeAnna if she had any family. She'd told him she had no one. Just now she'd told Rusty her grandmother always *says* a dog named is a dog claimed.

Says. Not said.

She'd mentioned her grandmother before, but always in the past tense. Just now she'd mentioned her in the present. Which probably meant her grandmother was still alive. *Then why had she told him she had no one? What was she hiding?*

With Chief resting comfortably in the front seat, Rusty and LeAnna again crawled in the back. Slowly Vince drove through the back streets of Millerton, his mind in turmoil as he tried to understand.

An approaching car lighted up the interior of his Mustang, and for a brief moment he met LeAnna's gaze in the rearview mirror. Her brown eyes were opened wide, her dark lashes casting shadows below her brows. Her eyes crinkled slightly at the corners, and although he couldn't see her mouth, he knew she was giving him a tremulous smile.

With blood thundering through his head, he somehow managed to pull his gaze back to the street in front of him. The ride to his old house took only a few minutes. Vince spent them trying to list all the reasons he should just drop Rusty and the dog off at Lettie's, and LeAnna off at his old place, and drive on home. It didn't take him long to realize his feelings for LeAnna had nothing to do with *reason*.

"If Vince drops me off first," LeAnna said to Rusty, "I can stay with Casey, and Lettie can help you settle Chief down for the night."

"I could do it myself," Rusty declared.

LeAnna raised her eyebrows at the boy's tone of voice. Casey had already started to go through what she called his *me do it* phase. If Rusty was any indication, it looked as if he'd go through it twice.

Before LeAnna could speak, Vince said, "Of course you could, Rusty. But Lettie was wringing her hands pretty good when we left, and I have a feeling it would make her feel better if you let her help. Besides, every now and then it's nice to have a friendly helping hand."

Even Rusty's mumbled response didn't detract from the awe that rendered LeAnna speechless. The depth of Vince's understanding shouldn't have surprised her. Yet it did. For reasons she didn't want to explore, it also left her with an inner sense of peace. There were still good people in this world. Vince Macelli was one of them.

He pulled into her driveway and stepped from the car. Tipping the seat forward so that she could climb out, he held out his hand.

Every now and then it's nice to have a friendly helping hand.

His words were still echoing through her mind as she slowly placed her fingers in his palm. The dome light bathed her in a soft glow. It reached as far as Vince's shoulders, and threw the rest of him in shadow. Even in the relative darkness, she caught and held his gaze as his strong fingers closed over hers.

She felt weightless as he effortlessly pulled her to her feet. She straightened, mere inches separating her body from Vince's. Attraction worked over her in waves, and her gaze strayed down to his mouth. She was so close, it would take only a subtle shifting of her body and she could touch her lips to his. It would take only a tiny kiss, and it could lead to so much more.

"Did Doc Masey fix up that dog?" Lettie called from the back door.

Startled, LeAnna swung around to face her neighbor, pulling her hand from Vince's at the same time. "Yes," she called, her voice sounding thin even to her own ears. "I'll let Rusty tell you the details."

Now that the spell had been broken, she said goodbye to Rusty. Meeting Vince's gaze once again, she said, "I'd better go inside."

Halfway to the back door, Vince's deep, clear voice stopped her movements. "LeAnna?"

She turned around slowly.

"Would you like to go for a drive, or maybe just talk sometime?"

Aware of Lettie and Rusty's presence, she swallowed, and slowly nodded her head. "When?"

One side of his mouth lifted slightly before he said, "Soon."

There was something almost enchanting in that one tiny word. It filled her mind and drifted through her chest. She tipped her head to the side and gave him an unconscious smile before turning on her heel and silently walking into the house.

Inside, Lettie said, "You know, LeAnna, I've been thinkin'. Rusty hasn't made any friends since he came to live with us, 'cept Vince. Now the boy's opening up to you. That stray dog might be exactly what Rusty needs. Maybe this here is a turning point for us all. Wouldn't that be somethin'?"

Without waiting for an answer, Lettie hurried out the back door. Calling out a goodbye, she ducked through the gap in the hedge.

For a moment, all LeAnna could do was stare at the place where she'd last seen her friend. She finally pulled herself from her musings long enough to check on Casey, who was sleeping soundly. Within moments, Lettie's words were back in her mind.

Maybe this here is a turning point for us all.

LeAnna's life had taken a major turn six and a half months ago. She wasn't sure she could handle any more.

She heard Vince's car back out of Lettie's driveway and wandered out to the kitchen. Crossing her arms at her chest, she stood gazing at the darkness beyond the small window. She stood there for several minutes before coherent thoughts began to form. It had only been an hour since she'd first heard the squeal of brakes, when Rusty's voice had rung out for her help, and she'd dropped the clean clothes into the makeshift basket and...

The clean clothes.

She spun around and headed down the steps. With the moon as her only source of light, she picked up the items she'd dropped an hour ago, and deftly began unfastening the rest from the sagging line.

"It's a little late to be doing laundry."

LeAnna turned around slowly as Vince materialized out of the shadows. She didn't flinch or gasp, although watching Vince walk closer caused her heart to beat a little faster.

"What?" he asked. "Dogs scare the living daylights out of you, but I don't?"

She heard the teasing lilt in his voice. Smoothing her hand over a faded towel, she said, "That dog caught me by surprise. You told me you were coming back. You said soon. And you always mean what you say."

She placed the towel in her makeshift laundry basket and reached for a pair of Casey's shorts. From the corner of her eye, she saw Vince unclip a tiny shirt. After they'd removed every item, LeAnna bent to pick up the basket.

"Do you have to go in right now?" he asked, laying his large hand on her shoulder.

Warmth from his hand seeped through her thin shirt. His fingers were callused, and LeAnna instinctively knew his grip could be strong when he wanted it to be. Now his touch was gentle.

She glanced at the house, at the light spilling out the screen door. She'd locked the other doors, and as long as she kept the back door in sight, she didn't see any harm in enjoying the summer night.

"Come on," Vince said in a hoarse whisper. "Let's go sit on the bench in front of the garage."

He took her hand, pulling her with him through the darkness, to the bench, a short distance away. Something about the quiet night, the feel of her hand in his and the moon lighting their way made LeAnna want to giggle. It made her feel young and almost carefree. She'd been young once, a long time ago. But she'd never been carefree.

It took only a moment to reach their destination. Whispering, LeAnna said, "I'd say you've done this before."

He didn't speak in a whisper, as she had, but his voice was nearly as quiet. "When Conor and I were kids, this used to be our meeting place."

LeAnna had heard Vince speak of Conor, and knew they were half brothers. She'd seen Conor in the diner and at Mara's party, and remembered thinking how much the two men looked alike. They were both on the tall side, both dark, and both had a brooding quality.

"You had to sneak through the dark to meet your own brother?" she asked, lowering herself onto the bench.

"Back then, we didn't know we were brothers. You see, LeAnna, you aren't the only one with secrets."

Her lips parted as she took a quick breath. Any mention of her secret made her nervous. When Vince made no move to continue, her tension lessened. "What kind of secrets do you have, Vince?" she whispered.

"Uh-uh-uh," he said. "Unless you want me to come right out and ask you about *your* secret, don't expect an answer about mine."

Vince watched the play of moonlight in her eyes as her gaze probed his. Barely breathing, he waited to see if she'd accept this change in their relationship. Over and over again, she'd told him she couldn't stay in Millerton. He'd thought the fact that she was just passing through meant they couldn't have a relationship. Tonight, when he watched her across the waiting room, he realized he was wrong.

He knew that the accident she'd been in two weeks ago was the only reason she was here. She'd been working at the diner nearly every day, and was probably saving every penny she earned so that she could leave. He'd told himself she wasn't the kind of woman he was looking for. He'd been wrong. She was exactly the kind of woman he wanted, needed. And if he'd only known her for a matter of a few short weeks, well, that was a few more weeks than he'd have had if she hadn't come into his life at all.

"I see," she finally said. After a short pause, she continued. "Basically, what you're saying is that we aren't going to talk about secrets. Yours or mine."

Vince hadn't thought about it quite like that, but he supposed that was true enough. Besides, he had a feeling she wouldn't tell him why she was running, no matter how often he asked. At least not yet.

"Basically," he said, mimicking her tone.

She stared at him for a long moment. Before his eyes, her lips raised, and she began to laugh.

"What's so funny?" he asked.

"I'm sorry, Vince," she answered. "It's just that you have *attitude* written all over you."

Vince heard the deep, throaty tones of her laughter. It was a sound he hadn't heard often. Each time it happened, a smile stole across his face. Each time, he felt like applauding. He felt like strutting. More than anything, though, he felt like taking her into his arms.

Before he could move, she said, "I think you'd make a wonderful friend. Just remember, friendship is all I can offer you."

Vince narrowed his eyes, feeling that *attitude* she'd mentioned puff up his chest. "I wouldn't be too sure about that, if I were you," he insisted.

Before his eyes, LeAnna's expression changed. She raised her chin and tucked her tongue between her teeth. After casting him a measuring look, she said, "I guess you're just going to have to trust me on this one."

She'd done it to him again. Thrown the word *trust* at him, as if it were the most natural thing in the world. Her nearness sent desire pulsing through his body, and her saucy grin and subtle humor nearly stole his breath away.

She was wearing a T-shirt and cutoff jeans. As usual, her hair was a riot of curls. Someone else might have thought she looked sixteen, but then, someone else might not see the glint in her eyes, the glint that gave her a maturity beyond her years.

Friendship was all she had to offer? He didn't think so. Not for a minute. Since no one had ever accused Vince Macelli of being a stupid man, he kept that particular thought to himself.

Fireflies flitted nearby as they talked. Without preamble, he rose to his feet. He told her goodbye, and told her he'd be back. Soon. She nodded, and he turned away quickly, because he wasn't sure he could keep from kissing her otherwise.

His long strides carried him over the remaining distance to his house in near-record time. Pushing through his own back door, he finally took a deep breath. It did nothing to relieve the primitive tension filling his chest. He nearly gave in to the urge to tip his head back and yell like Tarzan.

I guess you're just going to have to trust me on this one. The memory of LeAnna's words brought him up short, keeping him from giving in to the urge to wake up the entire neighborhood. It was the second time she'd thrown his own phrase up between them. If he delved deep enough, he could see the significance of her statement. She *wanted* him to trust her.

Vince had never trusted easily. His childhood hadn't allowed it. Yet he trusted LeAnna. It might be instinctive, but Vince knew he hadn't gotten this far in life without developing strong instincts.

Every time he saw her, the attraction was greater, the pull stronger. He knew darn well it wasn't one-sided. LeAnna *said* she couldn't stay. She *said* they could only be friends. At least that was what she said out loud. Her gaze said something else entirely. And her kisses, well...

Vince stopped short, a smile stealing across his lips. From now on, he was going to listen to what her eyes told him, what her kisses told him. After all, he liked *that* message a hell of a lot better than *goodbye*.

Earlier, he'd told himself he'd have to be content with having known her for a few short weeks. He'd told himself he'd consider himself lucky to have had whatever time he could with her. Now, he realized he didn't want a few stolen weeks. He wanted the rest of their lives. He just wasn't sure how he was going to accomplish that. One thing he knew for sure was that he didn't want LeAnna to leave Millerton.

He had to win her trust. He knew he couldn't do that by charging in and sweeping her off her feet—she wouldn't take kindly to that. What he'd like to do was woo her gradually, slowly making her his. Unfortunately, she'd made it plain she wasn't going to be staying in Millerton forever. That meant he didn't have an overabundance of time.

He was going to have to plan this carefully. He couldn't rush her, and he couldn't take forever. One thing he could do was pray she fell in love with him, so deeply and so completely she wouldn't want to leave. Ever.

LeAnna scooped up Casey's big ball and gently tossed it back his way. Rusty pretended to run for it, and Casey screeched with glee when he reached it first. Chief, Rusty's new pet, raised his head, watching the activities from the shade.

"See that?" Lettie asked. "That dog hasn't taken his eyes off Rusty all day. He's adopted him, he has. Bud was just sayin' this morning, he don't know why he didn't think of it himself. Why, every boy needs a dog."

As usual with Lettie, all it took was a slight nod of LeAnna's head and Lettie rambled on about something else. Listening with one ear, LeAnna looked around at the tiny backyard. Rusty, bless his heart, was playing with Casey, while Chief looked on. Lettie sat near LeAnna on the back stoop, and Bud and Vince were standing near the gap in the hedge, talking about God only knew what.

LeAnna couldn't help but remember the first night she'd been here. That night, Casey had fallen asleep, and she'd wandered aimlessly through the quiet house, counting floor tiles and windows, and feeling more alone than she'd ever felt in her life.

Casey's giggle and Bud's hearty guffaw drew her from her musings. This evening, her yard was far from quiet. And LeAnna was far from lonely.

Vince turned his head, his gaze shifting to hers. For a moment, laughter was still evident on his face. But as he looked at her, his expression changed subtly. She stared wordlessly at him, her heart pounding. He offered her one of his small, secret smiles, and slowly swung his attention back to Bud.

LeAnna was sure there was something different in the beating rhythm of her heart. She'd told Vince she'd like to be his friend. Watching him now, she still wanted that. But she was drawn to Vince in a more-than-friendly way. She couldn't fall in love with him. She couldn't.

In her twenty-six years, she'd thought she was in love twice—once in college, and once after. When both relationships ended in heartache, she'd decided the emotion was greatly overrated.

And then she'd met Vince. She'd never been more in tune with another person in her life. She wanted to be his friend, but was afraid she'd wind up wanting so much more. Watching Casey laugh and play in the evening sunshine, she knew she was in no position to offer more than friendship, and in no position to want more in return.

Bud and Lettie began making noises about going back to their place. "Rusty," Vince called. "There's still a little daylight left, if you want to work on that old motorcycle."

Rusty nodded. Calling to his dog, he slowly ambled away. Casey toddled after them.

"Oh, no, you don't," LeAnna declared, scooping him up before he made it to the hedge.

"Down," the boy admonished.

"No, sweetheart. You have to stay here with me."

LeAnna saw the tears coming, but not the tantrum. Casey twisted, trying to get free. His tears only lasted a minute, but his wails went on and on. Bud, Lettie, Rusty, Vince, and even Chief, all turned, staring as if they'd never seen the child before.

Vince watched the way LeAnna handled the boy. She didn't let him go, but she let him have his tantrum. With a wry grin, she raised her voice over Casey's and said, "My grandma would say he's pitchin' a holler."

Although Bud and Lettie had never heard the expression, they nodded their heads in agreement before following Rusty and his dog through the hedge. Vince figured the kid probably wouldn't stop yelling until *everyone* left the yard. Unfortunately, his feet wouldn't seem to move.

He gazed across the narrow span of backyard, straight into LeAnna's eyes. He'd told her he wouldn't ask questions about her past. Just now, she'd again referred to her grandmother in the present tense. The glow in her eyes told him she'd done it on purpose, thereby answering one of his questions without being asked. She was beginning to trust him.

Vince felt as if he'd just been given a gift, and suddenly he didn't want to leave. Raising his voice over Casey's wails, he said, "Do you want to take a walk with me? After you get Casey to bed, I mean."

Shaking her head, she answered. "I can't leave Casey here alone, even if he is asleep."

"I'll ask Rusty to sit with him for a few minutes."

"I don't think fifteen-year-old boys want to baby-sit. It ruins their image."

"I'll bribe him," Vince returned. "Come on, LeAnna. It's just a walk."

Casey's cries were losing their shrillness; his tantrum was winding down. Watching LeAnna, Vince thought her resistance was doing the same thing. He decided to take her silence as acquiescence; after all, she hadn't turned him down, either. He wouldn't always be happy with crumbs, but for now he felt like kicking up his heels.

"I'll help you-know-who with that motorcycle. But I'll be back, LeAnna."

He hadn't said *soon*. Glancing at the tender expression on LeAnna's face, he realized he didn't have to. She knew that was what he'd meant. He'd be back all right.

Vince could hardly wait.

Chapter Seven

LeAnna opened the door for Rusty after his first knock. Glancing behind him, she asked, "Where's Vince?"

"I don't know. He told me to be here at nine o'clock sharp and wanted me to tell you he'd meet you in the backyard."

"Oh." Her thoughtful expression turned into a wry grin as she asked, "What did he promise you in exchange for sitting with Casey tonight?"

Smiling a little sheepishly, he said, "Chrome wheels for the Honda. But, LeAnna? You won't tell anyone I'm *babysitting*, will you?"

She couldn't help but laugh. "Don't worry, Rusty. My lips are sealed."

She gave him a few instructions in case Casey woke up, adding, "But I doubt that'll happen. Unless he has a nightmare, he doesn't wake up until morning." Glancing around, she said, "There isn't going to be much for you to do. I'm sorry I don't have a television or a radio."

"No problem," he assured her as he pulled a rolled-up motorcycle magazine from his back pocket.

"I won't be long," she said, turning to go. At the door, she swung around again. "Oh, Rusty? One more thing—"

He cut in quietly. "I know. I'll lock the door."

She hesitated, then slowly opened the door and stepped out into the quiet evening. On the top step, she gazed around. It was already a little after nine, and with the sun nearly down, long shadows stretched across the grass. She eyed the gap in the hedge, expecting Vince to come walking through any second. As if of its own volition, her gaze slowly strayed over the backyard, automatically noting the bright blue ball Casey had played with earlier, and the red wagon parked nearby. Her gaze trailed over the sagging clothesline, and on to the whitewashed garage out back. Her gaze stopped there.

Vince was sitting on the attached bench, his elbows resting on the back, his legs stretched out in front of him. He was wearing blue jeans and a white cotton shirt. His hair looked darker than usual, as if he'd just stepped out of the shower. Even when he was in shadow, she couldn't help but notice the lofty angle of his chin.

Sidestepping the wagon, she started off in his direction. "You were right about that wagon coming in handy," she said quietly. "Casey loved riding in it when we went to the grocery store yesterday."

He nodded, but his eyes never left hers.

"Why are you sitting out here?" she asked, drawing closer. "Have you changed your mind about taking a walk?"

He crossed his ankles, as if he had all the time in the world. "I haven't changed my mind. This just seemed like the most natural place to meet you, that's all."

LeAnna remembered when Vince had told her he used to meet Conor here when they were kids. Obviously this was a special place to Vince. She felt honored that he'd want to share it with her, and she was beginning to realize that with Vince she felt that way often.

He removed his arms from the back of the bench and bent his knees, finally rising to his feet. Tipping his head toward the street, he said, "You walk that way to and from work every day. Come on—I'll show you a shortcut."

He took her hand in his and tugged gently, leading her through the shadows at the back of the lot and on into the yard behind them. "Vince, we're trespassing."

He made a sound low in his throat before saying, "The neighbors are used to it. Old man Fergusson used to give me hell every time he caught me, but he's mellowed out since then. 'Course, the fact that he can't see this far anymore probably has a lot to do with it."

"Vince, you're uncivilized."

He glanced at her, and she knew he'd heard the excitement in her voice. She felt breathless and invigorated at the same time, and she loved the feeling.

They ducked around an old shed and slipped through a row of pine trees in the next yard. Within seconds, they were on the sidewalk on the next street over.

"I always knew you had a wild side," she declared.

His steps slowed, and his voice, when it came, was filled with underlying sensuality. "You ever wonder how wild we could be together?"

Erotic images shimmered through her mind, warming her body. She hoped Vince didn't expect a reply, because she was at a loss for something to say. She couldn't very well tell him the truth, that she had dreamed about making love with him, that she'd woken up feeling warm and heavy and still wanting. But, looking into his eyes now, she couldn't lie to him, either. So she said nothing.

He matched her stride as they began to meander along the old sidewalk. Vince pointed out houses, relating bits of history about the families living there. She listened to every word, marveling at the way his voice dropped in volume, and the way his words brought the people who lived in this neighborhood to life.

He evoked strong emotions from deep inside her. Le-Anna couldn't remember ever feeling this way. She'd repeatedly told him she wouldn't be staying in Millerton. She knew that Vince wasn't a patient man, yet he'd made no demands on *her*. He knew she had a secret, but he'd respected her privacy. He'd let her stay in his house, and he'd fixed up an old wagon for Casey. He made her smile, had even made her laugh a time or two. He made her feel special, through and through.

Strolling down the sidewalk with him, she realized that of all the things he'd given her, she valued the time he spent with her the most. She'd done what she had to do for Casey, and she knew she'd do it all over again if she had to. But it felt good to be liked for herself, respected for who she was inside. He'd given her several gifts, from that *borrowed* wagon to the use of his house, but his greatest gift was the way he made her feel. She was a woman. With him, she felt like one. She wished there was something she could give back to him, but she didn't know what it could be.

An ice-cream truck turned the corner up ahead, its music reminiscent of simpler days. Glancing at a child who was hurrying toward the white truck, she thought that maybe there was something she could give to Vince. Maybe she could give him a few answers to the unspoken questions in his eyes.

"Look," she said. "They didn't have those in Los Angeles, at least not in the area where I lived."

Vince followed the direction of her pointed finger, her words filtering through his mind. He glanced at her expression, and found a gentle smile on her lips and a confident gleam in her dark eyes. Her mention of Los Angeles hadn't been a slip of the tongue. It had been her way of telling him a little about her past. LeAnna was still a woman of mystery, but she was beginning to trust him.

"So you went from mountain to ocean," he said quietly.

They continued to stroll along the quiet streets, but now it was LeAnna's voice that was at one with the night. "They're beautiful in totally different ways. Our mountain was majestic, the ocean was mighty. It's impossible to live near either without realizing where the true power lies."

Vince heard the emotion in her voice. She'd loved her mountain, but she'd loved the ocean, too. Millerton, Michigan, had neither. It was this town he wanted her to love, this town and him.

"Were you in L.A. during the riots?" he asked.

She nodded, and he felt an odd twinge deep in his stomach. "You must have been terrified."

"A lot of things in this life are terrifying, Vince."

His heart sped up; his breathing deepened. The thought of LeAnna living through the violence and chaos of that riot put a knot in his gut. The fact that she'd lived through worse things brought that knot to his throat.

Bit by bit, he was learning more about her. She was patient and stubborn. Good Lord, was she stubborn. She'd been raised in the mountains of Tennessee, and had obviously had medical training. Her grandmother was still living. Somewhere. Now he knew *LeAnna* had been living in Los Angeles. All in all, it was a helluva lot more than he'd known two weeks ago. He wanted to know so much more.

Up ahead, Vince saw a young child skip toward her house, an ice-cream cone in her hand. The white truck disappeared around a corner, and suddenly the night seemed too quiet. His time with LeAnna was ending too soon.

They were standing on the sidewalk near his new house. From his position, he could see the apple tree way out back.

LeAnna had told him a little about her past. Suddenly he wanted to tell her a little about his.

"Come here," he said quietly. "There's something I want to show you."

LeAnna heard the huskiness in his voice. Although she knew she couldn't afford to be distracted by romantic notions, the sound of his voice and the mere touch of his hand on her arm sent intense awareness through her.

She followed him around the side of his new house, and on into the backyard. Even in the fading light, she could see the different rooflines of the house, and the smooth carpet of newly planted grass all around. There was only one tree in the entire yard, a gnarled old apple tree with an abundance of new green leaves. Without saying a word, he led the way to that tree.

She watched as he ran his hand over the tree's bark, her eyes following the scars over two pairs of initials. *C.B.#1* had a scratch through it. Immediately below were the initials *V.M.#1.*

"Yours and Conor's?" she asked.

Vince nodded. "Conor grew up on this lot. His house burned down thirteen years ago, but it was old and run-down and hardly mattered. This apple tree was his most prized possession. If anything had happened to this, I think he would have really been upset.

"Both our fathers were rotten, but his was worse. As it turned out, good ol' Sam Bradley was my father, too. Only I didn't know it then."

LeAnna listened to the deep undertones in Vince's voice. He was staring at the initials on that tree, but she wondered if that was what he really saw. "When did you and Conor realize you were brothers?"

"Last summer. Thirty-one years ago, Sam Bradley got my mother pregnant, then married Conor's mother, who was also pregnant—with Conor. All my life I wondered why

LeRoy hated me. For years I thought there was something wrong with me. Now I know there was something lacking in LeRoy. He wasn't all bad, at least not at first. He married my mother because he thought he was strong enough to raise another man's child as his own. But jealousy ate away at his goodness, and he grew to hate me.''

Vince's voice was as quiet as pain. There were several things she didn't understand, things about his past, about his childhood and the way his earlier years had shaped the man he was today. But one thing she understood was pain. It was in his voice, and if she looked deep enough, it was in his eyes, too.

She laid her hand on his forearm. Squeezing gently, she finally drew his gaze. "Sam Bradley was even worse than LeRoy?" she asked quietly.

He nodded, telling her about the man who used to own this lot. Sam Bradley had fathered two sons, but he'd raised only Conor. LeAnna had heard Vince talk about his brother often enough to remember that he'd recently married a woman with two young sons.

"Tell me, Vince," she said quietly. "How does Conor treat Jimmy and Jason?"

"Like they were his own flesh and blood. In Conor's heart, I think they are."

Tears stung the backs of LeAnna's eyes as she thought about Vince's last statement. Statistics proved that people passed their childhood abuse on to their own children. Conor hadn't laid a hand on his new sons. Instinctively LeAnna knew that Vince wouldn't, either. Bekka's sons were lucky to have Conor as a father. Someday, Vince's children were going to be even luckier.

Awe filled her heart. Yet sadness lingered around the edges, because she knew it would be someone else's children Vince fathered one day. Not hers.

"It's going to be dark in a few minutes," she said. "I really should get back to Casey. Thank you for showing me this old tree, Vince. I'll never forget it." With that, she started back the way they came.

"I want to see you again."

His words slowed her steps, but she didn't stop completely. "Maybe we could go for another walk sometime," she said, trying to ease the strain of the sorrow in her voice.

"I was thinking more like going out to dinner."

"I don't think that would be a good idea...." she began. "That sounds too much like a date."

Vince stopped walking. "You can call it anything you want, but the fact is, I want to see you again."

Turning to face him, she said, "I thought you understood that I'll be leaving soon."

He heard a car turn the corner, but he didn't take his eyes off LeAnna as he said, "You're here now."

Vince watched as she glanced over her shoulder. Taking a deep breath, he waited for her reply.

"I can't leave Casey."

Her refusal wouldn't have surprised him. Her reason for it did. "Rusty would probably watch Casey for you again."

"It isn't that I don't trust Rusty. But I don't like to leave Casey in that house when I'm not there."

Once again, LeAnna had told him more than he'd expected. This time, her words sent an ominous sense of foreboding to the pit of his stomach. He knew she left her child with Lettie every day. The fact that she was nervous about leaving Casey at *her* place brought a sickening realization to Vince's mind. LeAnna wasn't just running from someone. She was guarding her child against lurking danger.

Every chivalrous instinct he possessed roared to life within him. LeAnna wasn't scared for herself. She was scared for her child. There was no reason for desire to uncurl deep inside him, no reason except that he wanted to protect her and

Casey. He was falling in love, and love and desire went hand in hand.

Wordlessly, LeAnna gazed up at Vince, wondering if he'd question her reasons for refusing to leave Casey. The tough-boy jut of his chin was clearly evident. His shoulders were squared; his hands were on his hips. He gazed back at her as if he weren't pleased with her answer, but he wasn't angry. Relief slowly filtered through her entire body.

She'd paid Rusty for mowing her lawn with the money she'd made from tips, and had turned her last paycheck over to Tom O'Malley for car repairs. In less than a week, she'd have enough money to pay for the rest of her bill. And she and Casey would be leaving. There were a lot of things she was going to remember about Vince. She didn't want to remember his anger.

The neighborhood had grown quiet, and for the first time, she noticed that the streetlights had come on. The artificial illumination made his hair appear darker, the grooves beside his mouth deeper. But it wasn't artificial light that was dancing in his eyes. It was honest-to-goodness desire.

"All right," he finally said. "We won't leave Casey. But I still intend to see you. Every chance I get."

She gloried in his honesty. As she gazed into his eyes, one moment stretched to two. He smiled, and she felt an answering grin steal across her lips. He knew she was going to leave, yet he wanted to see her anyway.

"Come on," Vince said quietly. "If we don't get back to your place soon, Rusty will have me agreeing to throw in a chrome exhaust pipe to match his chrome wheels."

"Vince, what am I going to do with you?" she asked quietly.

The laughter trailed out of his voice as he answered. "It's interesting that you asked, LeAnna, because it just so happens that I have a few suggestions."

She shook her head most of the way back to her house, thinking she had a few *suggestions* of her own. Since they were within plain view of the people inside their houses, she kept her suggestions to herself. They ducked around the row of pine trees and cut through old man Fergusson's backyard without saying a word.

Vince stopped at the bench in front of the garage. Placing his hand on her shoulder, he slowly drew her around. In a voice barely more than a whisper, he said, "I'll be back tomorrow night."

The brush of his lips along hers was his only goodbye.

She could practically feel his eyes on her as she made her way to the back door. With her key in hand, she turned, looking all around her. The backyard was empty. Vince was gone. But he was coming back tomorrow night. She'd see him again.

Soon.

Although it was dark outside, inside she felt as if the sun were shining.

"Casey, honey, leave some of the water *in* the pool." LeAnna spread a towel on the ground, far enough away from her mischievous child to stay dry, yet close enough to keep an eye on him as he played.

Droplets of water glistened off Casey's curls as he let out his first genuine screech of pleasure all afternoon. The temperature and humidity had been rising all week, making Casey and just about everyone else irritable and just plain cranky. The pool had been Vince's idea. He'd shown up with it last night, during one of his daily visits.

She'd filled the wading pool hours ago, letting the sun's rays warm the water to a more comfortable yet refreshing temperature. Wearing only a diaper and a generous slathering of sunscreen, Casey plopped to his seat in the pool, splashing the nearly lukewarm water in every direction.

LeAnna lowered to the towel nearby and flipped open the top of the bottle of sunscreen, squirting a generous portion of the lotion into her hand. She smoothed the cream over her shoulders and down her arms, imagining it was Vince's hand, instead of hers. Excitement tingled deep inside her, shimmering outward.

Closing her eyes, she realized she felt this way every time she thought of Vince. It had been a week since they'd taken their first walk. True to his word, he'd shown up in her backyard or on her front stoop often in the days since. He'd told her he wanted to spend time with her, and that was what he'd done. They'd bought fudge bars from the ice-cream man and pulled Casey through the neighborhood in that old wagon. More often than not, they sat on the bench out back and talked. If it had been another era, LeAnna would have said that Vince was *courting* her.

The word sounded old-fashioned and romantic. That was exactly the way Vince made her feel. His smiles were tender, and his touches fleeting, but his kisses always weakened her knees. Any other man would have taken things farther. Not Vince. She knew he was holding himself back, and she felt warmed. Not by the hot rays of the sun overhead, but from the inside, where thoughts of Vince made her yearn for something she couldn't have.

"Whuzat?"

Casey's question pulled LeAnna from her thoughts. "This is sunscreen, so we won't get burned," she said, continuing to apply lotion to every inch of exposed skin the skimpy bikini didn't cover.

While Casey went back to fastidiously emptying the wading pool, one-fourth of a measuring cup at a time, LeAnna flicked her hair behind her shoulders and raised her face to the sun. She leaned back on her forearms and bent one knee. The movement did nothing to relieve the yearning deep in her belly.

* * *

Vince nearly strangled on the breath that had locked in his throat. Late-afternoon sunshine pelted his body, but the sun wasn't to blame for the layer of sweat breaking out on his brow, or the heat pounding like war drums low in his body.

He saw LeAnna angle her face toward the sun as she took a deep breath. From his position thirty feet away, he watched her breasts rise and fall, and moved his hands over his knees. He'd always known she had a great body. Hadn't he dreamed of holding her, touching her, every night? His dreams hadn't done justice to the way she looked in the light of day, just as he knew his dreams could never do justice to the way she would feel.

Her skin was naturally olive-toned. In the sunshine, it took on a golden hue. Her legs were long and muscular. Her hips were narrow, her belly was nearly flat. The scrap of pink bikini she wore left little to the imagination, but then, his imagination didn't need any help, anyway.

She moved her hips and rotated her shoulders as if searching for a more comfortable position. There was no such thing as comfort in Vince's condition. All he could think about was the way LeAnna would feel if she moved that way beneath him. Unfortunately, thoughts like those didn't alleviate his *discomfort*.

Her bikini bottom rode several inches below her waist, and the top covered barely more than half her breasts. Her supple skin rippled slightly over every rib. God, the woman was thin as a willow switch, but her curves lacked nothing. Except his hands.

He knew he should make his presence known, but he was reluctant to call attention to the state *his* body was in. She noticed everything else. He doubted she'd miss that.

He'd taken a cold shower every night this week, but the problem unerringly returned. There was only one thing that would really help. One thing with one woman.

Drops of water landed on LeAnna's left shoulder. She welcomed the cool relief. She peeked through her lashes at Casey, thinking about joining him in the little pool. Maybe a splash in the wading pool would offset the heat converging inside.

Pushing herself to a sitting position, she brought her knees up closer to her body, encircling her legs with her arms. She'd only been in the sun for a few minutes, yet she felt inordinately warm. Of its own volition, her gaze trailed away from the pool, skimming over the clothes on the line, and on to the whitewashed garage.

Vince.

Her breath rushed through her parted lips as she breathed his name. His presence explained the heat coursing just beneath her skin, the ache centering deep in her belly. He'd been watching her. Somehow, her body had felt the caress of his gaze. LeAnna knew she shouldn't wish for it, yet she longed for the touch of his hand, of his mouth, and so much more.

Meeting his gaze, she asked, "How long have you been sitting there?"

He shifted on the bench before answering. "A few minutes. Long enough to appreciate a beautiful woman when I see one."

She felt a blush creep to her cheeks, and wondered if she was suffering from heatstroke. Not from the sun, from Vince.

"I was just thinking about getting in the pool with Casey. You should have worn your swimsuit, so you could join us."

"I don't own a swimsuit." He stood slowly, and her gaze took in every inch of him before climbing to his eyes. The man was in the throes of a strong desire. The knowledge sent renewed heat shimmering through her.

LeAnna wet her lips and watched him walk nearer. She'd tried to tramp down her response to this man since the moment she'd met him. Looking at him now, she understood why it had been so difficult. There was more than mere attraction between them. If circumstances had been different, she might have believed she'd found the man she'd always hoped for, the one man in the entire world she could hold on to.

He was looking at her much the way he'd looked at her every day this week when he'd come into the diner. He'd made no pretense of keeping their relationship a secret, but he hadn't broadcast it, either. Neither was his style. And LeAnna realized she was coming to like his style. In fact, sometimes she was afraid she was coming to love it.

She'd arrived in Millerton with no intentions of staying. She knew that hadn't changed. She couldn't leave behind any clues that might help Nick find her and Casey. She'd certainly never intended to leave behind a piece of her heart.

Chief barked from the next yard, the sound drawing LeAnna from her thoughts. "Dog," Casey stated.

"That's right," LeAnna said.

Casey grinned at his cleverness, and LeAnna answered with a heartfelt laugh. Her child was as normal as any little boy could be. He was innately sweet and impishly mischievous. She hadn't seen the demons in his big brown eyes in a long time, and prayed she never would again.

Rusty whistled for his pet, and Casey jabbered his friend's name. With humbling clarity, she realized she wasn't the only one who was going to miss these special people when they left. If only there were some other way....

Vince went down on his haunches, dangling his hands in the cool water. "I could make some instant tea," she said quietly.

She watched as he cupped his big hands, catching the water Casey dumped into his palms. "No thanks," Vince answered. "I think I'll go on home and take a shower."

He cast a sardonic look her way, and she smiled at his wry expression. He hadn't said *cold* shower, but she knew that was what he'd meant.

"I just stopped in to ask you what time you want me to pick you and Casey up for Bekka's baby shower tonight."

LeAnna rose to her feet, then blithely lowered to the ground next to the pool. She moved her fingers through the cool water, bringing them to her face and neck. Tiny rivers of water trailed down her throat. Closing her eyes at the cool sensation, she tipped her head back and said, "Mara asked me to help her set out the food, so I'd like to get there a little early. Would seven o'clock be okay with you?"

His silence drew her face around, her eyes coming up to study his face. His gaze had followed the droplets of water down her neck, between her collarbones and over the upper swells of her breasts. Her heart hammered just below the surface of her skin, exactly where he was staring. He was so still, his attention so riveted, she had to remind herself to breathe.

Casey jabbered in the pool. LeAnna barely heard. She wet her lips and finally found her voice. "I'm usually more of a coverup kind of woman. This bikini was in the bottom of one of the boxes of clothes Mara loaned to me."

His gaze finally climbed to hers, and she nearly drowned in the masculine expression in his eyes. "Don't apologize. It's perfect."

Suddenly, even the tiny scraps of material felt too confining. His eyes were sending her a private message, one she couldn't help but respond to. LeAnna had never been brash or provocative. With Vince, she'd have liked to try both.

"Keep looking at me like that, and all the cold showers in the world won't do any good," he said in a throaty voice.

Her eyes strayed to Casey, who turned in the water like a shiny little seal. Her child was the reason she'd arrived inadvertently in Millerton. And he'd be the reason she left.

She wished with all her heart that things could be different. Even if she ended up with a broken heart, she wanted to spend as much of her remaining time with Vince as she could.

"I'm looking forward to Bekka's party tonight," she said.

"I'm looking forward to *after* the party," he returned huskily.

LeAnna didn't reply, at least not with words. She knew Vince saw the answer in her eyes. He could hardly wait until after the party, after Casey went to sleep, when she and Vince would be alone. He could hardly wait to kiss her, and touch her. And neither could she.

Chapter Eight

LeAnna looked up from the punch she was ladling into cups, trying to at least appear to be listening to what Mara was saying. It wasn't easy to think about anything except the way Vince had looked at her a moment ago, before disappearing into the next room.

He'd arrived on her doorstep at seven o'clock sharp. She'd never seen him in dress slacks and shirt, but she'd seen that sexy swagger of his dozens of times. He'd smiled at Casey and planted his hands on his lean hips. He'd obviously gotten his desire under control. Only his eyes betrayed his ardor, and his eyes said *soon*.

Mara placed the last glass of punch on the tray. "Come on, LeAnna. Let's go watch Bekka open her gifts."

LeAnna plucked Casey from the floor and followed her friend. There was talking all around. Voices rose; laughter rumbled. She trailed behind Mara, serving punch to the guests, marveling at the fact that she recognized each person she saw. That was something everyone here took for granted. These people had grown up with one another, but LeAnna felt as if this quiet acceptance, this ordinary life, were a gift. She wasn't afraid here, was even beginning to feel as if she belonged. She had a sudden burning wish that it could always be this way.

Mara's shrill whistle split the air. Now that she had everyone's attention, she instructed the guests to take a seat. With Casey tucked on one hip, LeAnna continued serving the punch on the tray in her other hand. Bekka, today's guest of honor, looked up from the baby blanket she'd just opened. Smiling at LeAnna, she said, "Your baby is darling. Could I hold him?"

Though she'd seen them at the Memorial Day barbecue, until tonight, LeAnna hadn't met Mara's family. Bekka looked a lot like her sister. Although Bekka was more subdued, their eyes and hair were the same color, and there was no disguising the genuine love both of them had for children.

"Of course!" LeAnna said, smiling down at the expectant mother.

Casey went into Bekka's outstretched arms so willingly, LeAnna was amazed. She watched him grin up at Bekka, and laughed right along with Bekka and Conor as Casey "helped" tear into the next package. Her baby really was beginning to trust again.

She swallowed the lump in her throat. Blinking back tears brimming in her eyes, she continued to pass out glasses of punch to the jovial guests, thinking about that sign on the edge of town, the one that said Welcome to Neighborly Millerton. LeAnna happened to know it wasn't the town that was neighborly. It was the people. They were special indeed.

Her vision cleared as she recognized the long fingers curling around the last glass on the tray. Her eyes unerringly found their way to Vince's. The people of Millerton might be special, but Vince was the most special of all.

"How much longer do you want to stay?" he asked.

"Forever." She didn't speak the word out loud, but her lips moved over every letter.

The tears in her eyes intensified the look in his. He'd read her lips, and he knew what she'd meant. Ever since she'd taken that walk with him last night, she'd felt a change in the area surrounding her heart. She felt breathless and happy, and she knew why. She was in love. Tonight, after the party, she was going to tell Vince about the secret in her heart, about her and Casey and that letter she kept hidden beneath her mattress. When she was through, she was going to tell him she loved him. And then ...

A high-pitched screech split the air. LeAnna sucked in a breath and spun around. The tray dropped from her hands. With her heart beating in her throat, she ran to her child.

The room grew quiet as everyone stopped talking and turned to the screaming little boy. LeAnna was aware only of Casey and his needs. Bekka was doing everything in her power to console him, but he looked up at LeAnna, big tears rolling down his cheeks.

"Maaa-maaa!"

LeAnna wrapped her arms around him and murmured soft words of comfort. "There, there," she crooned. "I'm here, sweetheart. I'm here."

"I didn't mean to frighten him," Todd Miller said.

"I'm sure you didn't," LeAnna replied, meeting the man's gaze. Anything else she might have said caught in her throat as she looked at his face. Although Mara's brother, Todd, had friendly blue eyes and an impish grin, he also had sandy-colored hair and a reddish beard.

Just like Nick.

Casey's eyes were still huge and red-rimmed, but his crying had stopped. Voices rose as relatives and friends teased

Todd about pinching the baby. The joviality continued. LeAnna barely heard. She sank onto an empty chair, cradling her child's dark head in the crook of her neck. Casey hadn't been frightened like that in nearly four months. She'd wanted to believe he'd forgotten. Now she knew he hadn't, at least not subconsciously. She wondered if he ever would.

Her gaze strayed across the room. Vince was watching her, a worried expression in his eyes. Moments ago she'd told him she'd like to stay in Millerton forever. Now she realized she couldn't do that. She'd made a vow to her sister and her grandmother, a vow she intended to keep. Most important, though, was the vow she'd made to Casey. The vow to keep him safe. In order to keep that vow, she couldn't put down roots.

Looking at Vince now, she remembered when he'd said he was looking forward to *after* the party. She knew he had a strong desire. So did she. But there was more than desire between them. She'd wanted to make love with him, to demonstrate how deeply she cared for him. Now she knew she couldn't go through with it. She didn't know how she was ever going to make him understand. One thing she did know: She wouldn't lie to him.

Bekka finished opening her gifts, and Casey slowly relaxed. As often happened at baby showers, the conversation turned to babies, labors and deliveries. LeAnna found herself laughing in spite of herself as one couple after another regaled them with delivery room stories.

"What about you?" one of the friendly guests asked LeAnna. "How long were you in labor for Casey?"

LeAnna's mind raced; her thoughts spun. She glanced down at Casey, her gaze swinging to Vince.

She couldn't lie.

Taking a deep breath, she smoothed a curl off Casey's forehead. "There were complications, so this little trooper was born by cesarean section."

Vince felt his eyes narrow. His blood pounded through his brain like a galloping horseman. He'd seen the panic in the little boy a few minutes ago, and he'd sensed a change in LeAnna. But nothing had prepared him for her answer. He was no expert, but he knew enough about cesarean sections to know they were surgically performed. He'd seen nearly every inch of LeAnna's supple body not covered by that tiny scrap of material she called a bikini. Her abdomen was nearly flat, and the skin was tight and smooth.

Surgery left scars. There were no scars on LeAnna Chadwick's stomach.

What was she hiding? Wasn't the child hers? Looking at them now, Vince didn't know how that could be. Casey looked just like her, from his curls to his dark eyes to his devilish smile. Why would she say he'd been born by cesarean section? Why?

Each question sent renewed dread through him. He'd known she had a secret. He was beginning to think it was a lot bigger and more dangerous than he'd imagined.

The party went on all around him. Vince barely noticed. All his attention was trained on LeAnna and Casey. He'd had every intention of taking her in his arms later tonight, and ending up in her bed. These new questions rivaled with his desire. But they didn't eliminate it.

A few minutes ago, LeAnna had insinuated she wanted to stay here in Millerton forever. God, he could still remember the way her lips had moved over that word. Now, she'd pulled up into herself, wrapping her cloak of secrecy around herself and Casey. He instinctively knew the evening wouldn't end the way he'd planned. He also knew LeAnna must have good reasons for keeping her secret. He was beginning to think her reasons had to do with life or death.

He wanted her to stay in Millerton. He wanted her to trust him with the secrets of her past. He'd made light of it before, telling himself that everyone had their secrets. Vince didn't plan to make light of it anymore. If she was in danger, he wanted, needed, to help her.

Not caring who heard or saw, he strode to her side. Clasping her hand in his, he said, "We have to talk."

She turned her face toward his, and he didn't like what he saw in her eyes. He didn't like the worry between her brows, or the glimmer of unshed tears. Most of all, he didn't like the shadows he saw in the places her desire had been.

LeAnna glanced at Vince's profile as he pulled his car into her driveway. His mouth was set in a straight line, and a muscle clenched in his jaw. With all her heart, she wished she could stay in this town, with this man. She swallowed against the sob filling her throat as one of her grandmother's old sayings filtered through her mind. *Wishing don't make it so, LeAnna. It never has, and it never will.*

Vince walked around to her door and reached for Casey. The action took her by surprise, and before she could stop herself, she flinched. It took incredible effort to meet Vince's eyes, even more to hold his gaze.

"I wouldn't hurt Casey. Ever."

Tears stung the backs of her eyes as she whispered, "I know you wouldn't. I'm sorry."

Of course Vince wouldn't hurt Casey. Sometime during the past week, she'd realized she loved him. She trusted this man, had been ready to entrust him with her body. Tonight's party hadn't changed her trust, but it had changed the outcome of the night.

LeAnna had wanted to rid herself of her secret, to tell Vince everything. But Casey's reaction to Todd Miller kept her from doing so. Before they left the party, Vince had told her he wanted to talk. She knew he'd seen Casey's terror, and *she'd* seen Vince's eyes narrow when she told everyone that Casey had been born by cesarean. Vince Macelli wanted answers. The fact that he wasn't demanding them made her love him even more.

They walked side by side toward the back door, not quite touching, yet wanting to. She tried not to think about how different it might have been if Casey hadn't been afraid of Todd Miller, if his scream hadn't reminded her of how he'd looked seven months ago, how he'd whimpered, too frightened to cry, too pitiful not to.

"Vince! LeAnna! Thank goodness you're back!" Lettie ducked through the hedge, wringing her hands. "I'm home alone, and I just don't know what to do!"

"What's wrong?" LeAnna asked as the other woman hurried closer.

"He found him. I saw him. What are we gonna do?"

LeAnna gasped. She clutched Casey tighter and cried, "Who, Lettie? Who did you see?"

"It was that man, that awful man. He's evil, he is. And I don't know what he'll do to Rusty if he catches him."

Lettie's words sank into LeAnna's mind, and realization dawned. Lettie hadn't seen Nick. She was afraid of someone else.

"I know they were members of that gang. I just know they were. How did they know Rusty was here? How did they find us?"

"Where's Rusty?"

Both women turned to look at the man who'd asked the question. Vince's eyes were narrowed as he waited for Lettie's answer. His back was perfectly straight and his shoulders were squared, as if he were ready to jump into action at any given moment.

Running her fingers across her white knuckles, Lettie said, "I don't know. Rusty saw the car out the window and took off across the backyard half an hour ago. I haven't seen him since."

"Did the man in the car see Rusty?" Vince asked.

"There were three of them, but I don't think they saw him," Lettie answered, calmer now.

"Good," Vince replied. "Rusty is a smart boy. He'll stay out of sight. Remember, this is his town. He knows it backward and forward. They don't. You say there were three of them? Can you describe them?"

Lettie took a shuddering breath, but she couldn't speak.

LeAnna moved closer. She removed her hand from Casey's back and placed it on the other woman's arm, quietly saying, "It's going to be all right, Lettie. Vince will find Rusty. I know he will."

Chief, Rusty's dog, let out a long, mournful howl that sent shivers down LeAnna's spine. Casey began to whine, and Lettie said, "I hope you're right. I just never thought they'd find Rusty here. He never told them about us, so how did they know?"

Vince began to ask questions, and Lettie described the gang leader as best she could. "I heard one of them call the driver Guido. They were all wearing black coats, even though it's hot out. Their hair was slicked away from their faces, and they all wore the same color of bandannas. Rusty has one just like it up in his room."

Vince said, "You think these are the guys who beat Rusty to a pulp because he wouldn't do everything they said?"

Lettie nodded. "I don't know why they beat him up. Rusty's never wanted to talk about it. But I think it's the same guys, Vince. What if they kill him this time? Why else would they have come?" Her voice rose to near hysteria, breaking off convulsively on the last word.

"He was smart enough to get away from them before, Lettie. He'll do it again."

"Vince is right, Lettie," LeAnna said, rushing to reassure her friend. "I've seen Rusty run like the wind. I don't think they'll find him."

"I pray you're right," Lettie replied, her voice slightly steadier now. She turned back toward her house, and Vince turned to go. Approaching headlights froze everyone to the spot.

"It's Bud," Lettie cried in relief. "Vince, you see if you can find Rusty. I'll tell Bud what's goin' on."

Jiggling Casey, LeAnna watched Vince go. From inside his car, he said, "I'll be back."

Even in the tension-filled situation, he hadn't forgotten her. It sent a flash of wild grief poking through her, leaving her with a feeling of incredible emptiness.

She unlocked her door and strode inside, where she automatically changed Casey and buttoned his summer pajamas. Usually he fell asleep as soon as they were settled into the rocking chair. Tonight he was fretful, difficult to console. She had a feeling there was more to it than simply being overtired. Seeing Todd Miller had jarred his subconscious memories. He was terrified, and he was too young to understand why.

She walked through the quiet house, her swaying strides gradually lulling him to sleep. After singing him his favorite lullaby, she lowered him into his bed and lovingly tucked a lightweight blanket around him. Next she washed her face and brushed her teeth and hair, then slowly strolled through each room, counting light switches and floor tiles, windows and registers, waiting for Vince to return.

A few hours ago, she'd been daydreaming about her life here. In her imagination, she and Vince would marry and raise Casey. They'd live in his new house and it would be a real home. She'd thought about the flowers she'd plant near the front and back doors. She doubted if mountain laurel would grow in Michigan, but rhododendrons would, and azaleas and goldenrod.

For a brief time, she'd fantasized about staying. When Casey had been frightened of Todd Miller, her fantasies had wobbled like a tower of blocks in the wind. When Lettie had said, *"He found him,"* those fantasies had come crashing down around her. She'd thought Lettie meant Nick. The fact that she hadn't didn't chase away LeAnna's unease. She was worried about Rusty, but she was worried about Casey, too. If that gang had found Rusty, Nick could find her. She didn't want to keep running, but she didn't know what else to do.

Headlights flickered through the darkness, and gravel crunched beneath tires. Automatically she stayed in the shadows and looked out the window. Recognizing the black Mustang pulling into the driveway, she sighed in relief.

Vince was stepping from his vehicle when she walked out to the front stoop. "Did you find him?" she asked.

He shook his head. "Not a sign of Rusty, or the car Lettie described."

Vince dropped down to the middle step and sat statue-still, waiting to see if she joined him. Her shoes scudded quietly on the wood landing. Moments later her soft aqua skirt brushed his arm on her way down. A moth fluttered near the porch light, and a night breeze blew through the trees. Otherwise, the neighborhood was quiet.

Vince was aware of every move LeAnna made, from the way she folded her arms to the way she straightened her spine. Her face looked pale, and there were smudges beneath her eyes. They intensified the air of fragility surrounding her. She looked bone-weary, as if she carried the weight of the world on her shoulders. How could he make her see that she didn't have to carry it alone?

"LeAnna?" he asked in a choked whisper.

Slowly she raised her gaze to his.

"Does Casey's father have sandy-blond hair and a beard?"

For a long moment, she simply gazed back at him. She finally nodded, and in the ensuing silence, Vince called himself every kind of fool. He was lousy at relationships, always had been. Still, he wanted to have a relationship with LeAnna. He wanted her to trust him, confide in him.

He drew his knees up closer to his body, resting his elbows on his thighs. "I know you're running from him. I think I know why. There are a lot of things about you I don't understand, but I know you'd never do anything bad. I trust you. And I want you."

LeAnna listened to the deep tones in Vince's voice. Warmth coursed through her, from her cheeks, down her shoulders, through her breasts and on to her toes. Being wanted by Vince Macelli was a powerful stimulant. She knew what he wanted, and it was more than her body. He wanted her to open up to him, to tell him the truth. Her breath came in shallow gasps, and she realized she wanted the same thing. She lowered her eyes and took a deep breath, trying to find the proper words to convey her feelings.

A car slowly turned the corner. They both watched it advance, silently recognizing it as the car Lettie had described. It inched its way along the street, and Vince could make out three heads inside. Three, not four. That meant they hadn't found Rusty.

He'd never realized how many different kinds of anticipation there were, and he'd never known a man could feel so many of them at one time. He'd anticipated taking LeAnna in his arms since the day he'd met her. His muscles had tensed with need countless times. He was worried about Rusty. What an understatement. He wanted to protect the people he loved, but felt ill equipped to do so.

Vince's back stiffened as the car pulled to a stop at the curb directly in front of him. His tension coiled tighter and his fingers flexed as a greasy-haired punk who looked old enough to know better rolled his window down and spat.

"Hey!" he called. "We're lookin' fo' a friend of ours. 'Sposed to live around here. Name's R.J. You seen him?"

LeAnna laid her hand on Vince's arm, momentarily drawing his gaze. He watched her ease into a demure smile as she said, "R.J., you say? I've been living here all summer, and I haven't met anybody named R.J. Are you sure he lives in Millerton and not Midland or Middleton?"

The punks exchanged words inside the car. Without another sound, the window was rolled up and the car pulled away. It ran a stop sign and squealed around a corner. Vince heard it shift into third, its engine fading away as it headed south. Away from Millerton.

Two long sighs filled the quiet night.

"Do you think they'll come back?" she asked.

Vince shrugged, watching as LeAnna smoothed a wrinkle from her full skirt. He was more than a little amazed at the ease with which she'd handled those boys' questions. She was a master at evading an issue, at leaking out only half the truth. He'd always known it, but never as clearly as at this moment.

The breeze blew her blouse against her skin. Vince's gaze followed the gently fluttering material. The top was sleeveless and scoop-necked, the aqua color bringing out the richness of her skin. Her hair looked recently brushed, the porch light reflecting off the waves like a halo. He happened to know LeAnna was no angel. She was evasive, downright sneaky. If lies of omission were really lies, she'd lied plenty. Only LeAnna hadn't lied, not really. She hadn't told him the whole truth, but then, she'd never pretended to.

"Do you trust me, LeAnna?"

She raised watery eyes to his, but she didn't answer. She didn't have to. He saw the answer in her eyes, in the tears she wouldn't let fall, in the tenderness in her expression, and in the way her lips trembled as she tried to smile. She trusted him. The knowledge filled his heart and gave him hope.

He leaned closer, closer, until his lips were but a breath away from hers. "Then tell me," he murmured against her mouth. "Tell me, so I can help."

"I love you," she whispered against his mouth.

He felt, more than heard, her words, felt them against his mouth, and in his heart. Her kiss worked magic on his body, her words worked magic inside it. He'd wanted the truth. She'd given him something even more precious.

His hands cupped her shoulders, pulling her closer. Her arms slid around his waist, the desire between them harmonizing like two voices singing the same slow song. He kissed the pulsing hollow at the base of her throat, then followed a trail to her collarbone. She brought her hands to his hair, kissing his forehead, his temple, finally bringing his face back to hers, as if she needed his kiss more than her next breath.

Out of nowhere, a piercing cry jerked them apart. They both stiffened, but she was the first to find her feet. The sound came again. Shrill. Anguished. Hysterical.

LeAnna's face went pale, her eyes a little wild. "I'm coming, Casey. I'm coming," she murmured in a tear-choked voice. "Don't be afraid. I'm coming."

Chapter Nine

LeAnna moved like lightning, up the steps and into the house. The screen door slammed before Vince could stop it. He stood, too, swore under his breath, and walked inside.

Casey was still crying in the next room, but he no longer sounded hysterical. Vince heard LeAnna's low, smooth voice as she comforted the baby. A short time later, she came out of the bedroom, her arms wrapped tightly around her child.

"He's had a nightmare," she said solemnly.

Vince felt a shudder go through him. What sort of trauma caused a child so young to have this kind of nightmare? Good Lord, what had this baby been through?

Breathing deeply, he gazed at LeAnna. She seemed to have the situation under control, but he saw the way her hand shook as she patted Casey's back. She was so strong, and she was always there for Casey. If it took him a hundred years he intended to show LeAnna that he'd always be there for her. Problem was, he didn't have a hundred years. Neither of them did.

Without saying a word, he turned and walked back out to the front stoop. He lowered himself to the bottom step. And waited. He struggled with his thoughts. His head pounded, his heart thudded, and he was sure he'd never felt so helpless or so wretched, not even when LeRoy had struck him, or when Conor had cleared out of town all those years ago.

A child's lullaby carried to his ears, and tears stung his eyes. The boy's whimpers gradually ceased. Never in his life had Vince felt such an onrushing of emotion, such an enormous sense of awe, at one quiet woman's inherent strength.

Somewhere a dog barked and a door slammed. Other sounds came from inside the house, quiet sounds he recognized from living there most of his life. In his mind's eye he saw LeAnna walk into his old bedroom. He imagined her lithe movements as she lovingly tucked Casey into his bed again. After a time, the screen door creaked open. Vince stood, and slowly turned around.

"Is he all right?" he asked.

She nodded sadly.

"This isn't the first time he's had this dream, is it?"

After interminable seconds, LeAnna shook her head. "There's something I have to tell you, Vince."

An ominous sense of foreboding crawled down his spine. "You know you can tell me anything."

She met his gaze and quietly said, "Casey and I will be leaving at the beginning of the week."

Her quiet voice was at odds with the death grip she had on the railing. It left Vince feeling raw. He nodded, but he didn't say a word. He just pried her fingers from the railing and, one by one, kissed each white knuckle. She pulled her hand back slowly, just as a huge tear rolled down her cheek.

"You'll tell me when you find Rusty?" she asked.

"I'll have Lettie let you know when Rusty comes home. Don't worry about him. My gut instinct tells me he's okay."

It was her turn to nod. "I'll probably always worry, you know. About all of you."

Vince wasn't a man who was comfortable with his emotions, especially his tears. He choked down a sob and forced the moisture from his eyes. He hadn't cried in years, not even when the man he'd thought was his father had died. This was different. LeAnna Chadwick had busted into town and changed his life. Her leaving would forever change him.

"Will you tell me goodbye before you leave?" he asked quietly.

"I'll try."

Vince knew it was as good as she could do. With a slight nod of his head, he turned around and hurried toward his car. Halfway there, he saw a firefly flicker out of his reach. Just as LeAnna was about to do.

"Whuzat?"

LeAnna tried to instill her voice with happiness as she pointed to the black nose poking through the hedge. "You know what that is. That's Rusty's dog, Chief."

"Chief."

Casey watched the gap in the hedge, because he knew Chief was never far from Rusty's side. Sure enough, the strawberry-blond teenager ducked through seconds later. Chief, who was getting fairly adept at walking on three legs, stood guard at his side.

LeAnna continued picking up toys in the backyard as she said, "Well, hello, Rusty. You're not looking too bright-eyed or bushy-tailed this morning."

"I could be looking a lot worse."

LeAnna couldn't bring herself to return his sheepish grin, and Rusty averted his gaze. "Guess everyone was pretty worried about me, huh?"

"I think your grandma has a few more gray hairs this morning, but we're all just glad you're all right. Lettie said you found a pretty good hiding place," she stated, referring to the apple tree in Vince's backyard.

Rusty winced. "If anybody hears about that, I'll never make it at this high school."

LeAnna remembered what it was like to be fifteen, to want to be popular, to wish for nice clothes and dates with the most popular boy in school. She guessed she hadn't changed all that much since her teenage years. Today she found herself wishing for a life with the most handsome, virile and compelling man in Millerton.

"I don't think you have anything to worry about," she answered. "The only people who know that you hid in that tree house are your grandparents, and me, and Vince. Bud and Lettie are so relieved to have you back, they'd never say anything. I won't tell a soul, I promise. And Vince doesn't say much."

"No, but what he says, he means."

LeAnna looked at the boy. He was on the verge of manhood, really, and in many ways, what he'd been through in Detroit had made him mature beyond his years. She watched as he tossed the big blue ball across the yard at Casey. Chief plopped down in the shade, and Rusty looked at the ground. Shifting from one foot to the other, he finally looked into her eyes. "Uh..." he began.

"What is it, Rusty?" she asked.

"Do you have to be at the diner right away?"

Shaking her head, she said, "Since today's Saturday, I'm only working the lunch crowd for Trudy. I don't have to leave for an hour. Why?"

"I've never talked about what happened to me before I came to live with Grandpa and Grandma. Vince said you'd understand."

So, Rusty had talked to Vince. The knowledge that they both believed in her capacity for understanding lingered around the edges of her mind as she quietly waited for Rusty to continue.

Rusty began to speak, his voice crackling with fatigue and emotion. "I got beat up real bad. I didn't think the guy was going to stop until I was dead. A person doesn't forget something like that, ya know?"

LeAnna nodded solemnly. "I know, Rusty."

"Vince said he heard Casey scream last night. Did someone beat you and Casey, LeAnna?"

LeAnna smoothed her hands down the kelly-green shorts she was wearing, her eyes following her child's progress across the backyard. Casey was trying to pick up the ball, but every time he got close, his little foot got in the way and he ended up kicking it out of his reach.

Motioning to indicate Casey's antics, she said, "You wouldn't have recognized him seven months ago, Rusty. He was skinny and bruised and terrified of the dark. His father only laid a hand on me one time. Casey wasn't that lucky. I'd planned to do everything legally and sue for sole custody. But when I walked into that room that night and saw Casey, I knew I couldn't wait. He was just a baby. By morning, he'd have been dead. So I took him and ran. The last thing Nick said to me was that he'd find me if it took forever."

LeAnna turned her head so that she could look directly into Rusty's eyes as she continued. "And when he does, he'll kill me. He wouldn't kill Casey right away. But Casey's death would be even more brutal, because he'd die one day at a time."

"His name is Nick?"

She nodded. "Nick Calhoun."

"How did you ever get mixed up with a guy like that?" Rusty asked. "I mean, you seem too smart to be with a jerk like that, even one time."

A blush rose to Rusty's cheeks when he realized what he'd said. LeAnna smiled a sad smile, her gaze following Casey as he chased a butterfly across the backyard. "I didn't get mixed up with him, Rusty."

"But if you're Casey's mother..."

LeAnna thought about the letter she'd hidden beneath the mattress the first night she was here. "I am Casey's mother in every way that matters. But I didn't give birth to him. My sister did."

Rusty's mouth dropped open as a look of understanding slowly settled over his features. "Where's your sister now?"

LeAnna felt the warm breeze on her cheeks. It rippled through her curling hair like a whisper and a caress. She looked up into the sky, where gray clouds were beginning to gather, far in the east.

"I like to think Karlie's in heaven," she answered. "But sometimes, I could swear she's right here with me."

For a long time, LeAnna had grieved for her sister in silence. Recently, she'd told Vince a little about Karlie. And now she'd told Rusty. Each time she talked about Karlie, LeAnna felt better. It was as if the hurt were fading, and the love lived on.

Lettie had told LeAnna that she was worried that Rusty wasn't happy in Millerton. Since she would be leaving soon, LeAnna wanted to tell her young friend to be patient, that this town would grow on him if he gave it a chance. "Your grandma said you lived here until you were seven, and then moved to Detroit with your mother. What do you think of Millerton, now that you're back?" she asked.

"Compared to Detroit, it's pretty boring. But it's safe, I guess."

"Safe isn't a place, Rusty," LeAnna said quietly. "It's a feeling."

He began to talk, his words forced at first, but gaining momentum as he told LeAnna about his life in Detroit. He didn't know where his father was, and his mother had gotten mixed up with the wrong people. He said she wasn't very strong. So he'd turned to a gang, wanting more than anything to belong.

"At first it was great. I had a family, a brotherhood, ya know? But as weeks went by, I started to notice things they did. I never said anything, but one of the older guys, Guido, didn't like it that I saw. He hated me. I guess he didn't need a reason. He was bigger, and itching for a fight. One day I got tired of taking it. He all but beat the life out of me. That ain't belonging, LeAnna, ya know?"

"I know, Rusty," LeAnna said. "I saw hundreds of boys like that in L.A. Every once in a while, I saw one like you. Someone strong enough to rise above, smart enough to get out, brave enough to go on."

"You really think I'm all those things?" he asked shyly.

"I know you are. I only wish I could stick around and see for myself what a wonderful man you're going to turn out to be."

"Then you're leaving?" he asked.

She nodded. "I have to, Rusty. I don't want to. But I have to."

"Are you coming back someday?"

"What do you mean?" she asked, her voice sinking lower as she contemplated his question.

"I mean, when it's safe. Are you coming back then?"

She'd never thought of that. Could she come back here one day? She and Casey?

Thoughts formed in her mind, one on top of the other, making it difficult to concentrate on any one idea. Was there another way? Could she gain legal custody of Casey without jeopardizing his life? In her jumbled confusion, one word repeatedly filtered through her mind. *Vince*.

"Rusty, are your grandparents going to be home tonight?"

The teenager eyed her quizzically before shaking his head. "There's a superbingo going on in the social hall. Grandma says they're going as soon as you pick Casey up after work."

"Oh."

"You have an idea, don't you?" he asked.

LeAnna nodded slowly. "I need to talk to Vince."

"I knew it," the boy answered. "I'll watch Casey for you, on one condition."

She grinned at his wry expression.

"You can't tell anyone I'm a baby-sitter."

"It's a deal," she said. Hope and anxiety mingled in LeAnna's chest as she watched Rusty and Chief amble back to their side of the hedge. She finished picking up Casey's toys, her mind racing ahead to what she planned to tell Vince.

"Book," Casey exclaimed, toddling toward her.

"Did Rusty drop his magazine?" she asked, carefully pulling the motorcycle digest from Casey's chubby fingers. "We'll give it back to him later. Let's go change your diaper and get you ready so you can go over to Rusty's."

Inside, she slid the magazine on top of the refrigerator and dropped the toys she'd collected from the backyard into a box in the living room. She changed Casey's clothes and slipped into her pink waitress uniform, a prayer on her lips the entire time.

She didn't think she could risk taking Casey back to Tennessee to gain sole legal custody of him. After all, Nick would never stand for that. He'd rather kill his own child than let her have him. And LeAnna would never let that happen. Never. What alternative did that leave her? She couldn't risk staying in Millerton, either. What if Nick traced her here?

She'd only been here a little over three weeks, and already she wanted to stay forever. Rusty had asked if she'd come back someday. LeAnna knew she'd like to believe she could. No matter what happened, there was one thing she had to do. She had to tell Vince the truth. Even if she never saw him after this weekend, she wanted him to know.

A cat darted around the corner of the building as Vince eased into the alley behind the Grady Motel. He automatically glanced at the dented trash cans lining the dilapidated chain-link fence out back, but saw nothing that looked suspicious.

Someone had called about a disturbance. That wasn't unusual for this place. What *was* unusual was his nagging suspicion that something wasn't quite right.

He'd been preoccupied ever since LeAnna had called him at the station. Her voice had wavered over the phone lines, and Vince had had a sinking suspicion that she was going to say goodbye. He was working a crazy shift this weekend, but he'd agreed to meet her at his place at seven.

Vince pulled the patrol car around to the side of the old motel. Skirting broken glass, he eyed the neon sign someone had busted. He caught a movement out of the corner of his eye and swung around. A torn drapery fell into place, leaving Vince with the hazy impression of a bearded man.

Old man Grady opened the front door and slowly ambled toward him. The man had thinning hair and was carrying at least a hundred pounds of extra weight. When Vince was a kid, he'd thought Grady had shifty eyes. His opinion hadn't changed in the years since.

"What's the problem, Macelli?" Grady asked.

Vince cast a careful look all around, then stepped out of the car. "I just received a call that there was a disturbance out here."

"A call from who?" the man asked, his eyes nearly disappearing as he squinted.

"The person didn't leave his name."

"I ain't heard no commotion. Musta been a false alarm," Grady jeered.

"You haven't noticed anything unusual going on?" Vince asked, trying to keep his voice level.

"Nope," Grady insisted. "Looks like somebody's been wasting your time."

Vince strode through the door and looked around. The place was as run-down as it always was, but nothing looked amiss. "Have you noticed anybody strange lurking around lately?"

His question was met with an icy stare. Vince asked a few other questions, not because he expected answers, but because it was his job.

The place was a hole. Thank goodness LeAnna and Casey hadn't stayed here the first night they were in town. The thought of them sleeping out here turned his stomach. The thought of them leaving made his whole body ache.

He crawled behind the steering wheel and left the parking lot, his mind in turmoil. He'd lain awake long into the night last night, trying to think of some way to convince LeAnna to stay. If there was a way, he sure as hell hadn't thought of it. Maybe that was why he'd woken up with a bothersome headache, and a dull ache of foreboding.

At seven o'clock he pulled into his own driveway, and found LeAnna on her knees near the corner of the house. The sight of her relieved the pressure in his chest, but it didn't help the pressure anyplace else.

"You're probably wondering what I'm doing," she said with a smile.

"The thought crossed my mind."

She patted her gloved hands over the soil surrounding some sort of flowering bush. Continuing with her project, she said, "Your house is lovely, Vince, really it is. I couldn't find any mountain laurel, but these rhododendron plants are beautiful, don't you think?"

Vince didn't give the plants much attention, but he hoped the fact that she was planting them meant she was putting down roots. "They're okay. But why are you planting them here?"

She stopped packing the soil around the bushes and looked up at him. "Because your house needs a woman's touch."

He took a step closer. "What if I told you I needed the same thing?"

LeAnna rose to her feet slowly, Vince's words pulsing between them. She removed her gloves and finally met his gaze. "That's what I want to talk to you about."

She dropped the gloves into the wagon and brushed the blades of grass off her blue cotton skirt. Glancing all around, she noticed the apple tree out back. Rusty had hidden from danger in its branches, and Vince had told her about his childhood beneath them. It seemed like the perfect place to tell Vince the truth.

"Let's talk," she said. "There."

Even though she'd been rehearsing what she'd say all day, they reached the tree in silence. Now that the moment of truth had arrived, she was at a loss for words. How could she tell him what knowing him had given her? How could she put into words the way his belief in her had helped heal her battered heart?

Although the sky was filled with dark clouds, the air felt cooler beneath the old apple tree. She tipped her head back so that she could gaze up through the leafy branches. "That's quite a tree house," she said quietly.

"Nothing but the best for Conor's boys. If Casey were a little older, I'd give him a guided tour."

She turned her head so that she could see Vince. He was leaning against the tree trunk. One leg was bent at the knee, and both hands were in his pockets. As he had been the first time she'd met him, he was wearing his badge.

"You've already given Casey so much," she whispered.

"Did he sleep okay last night?"

LeAnna nodded. "Like a lamb. You know, I'll never forget the first time I saw him. He was minutes old, and he looked up into my eyes and I was lost. Karlie always teased me about it. She said Casey always had me wrapped around his little finger."

After a long silence, Vince asked, "Karlie's the one who had the cesarean section, isn't she?"

After barely a moment's hesitation, she inclined her head slightly and asked, "Did Rusty tell you?"

"No. I just believed you were telling the truth. About everything. And I put two and two together. Besides, you're too levelheaded, too intelligent and strong, to let yourself get mixed up with someone like Casey's father."

"Sometimes it's more a matter of luck than brains," she whispered. "In Karlie's case, it was bad luck."

LeAnna turned her body so that she was at a ninety-degree angle to Vince. With the pad of one finger, she slowly traced the weathered outlines of the initials two young boys had carved into the tree a long time ago. Conor Bradley, number one. Vince Macelli, number one. As it turned out, both boys had grown up to be wonderful men. In LeAnna's heart, though, Vince Macelli really was number one.

"When I first left the mountain, I thought it was just a matter of time before Grandma and Karlie would come to live with me in California. Grandma and I had talked about it often, and I'd made plans to take a week off and come get them. But then Karlie met Nick. Before long, she was pregnant, and wouldn't even talk about leaving.''

Vince stayed perfectly still, listening to the soft cadence of LeAnna's speech. He heard the tremor in her voice as she told him about the first time she'd seen bruises on her sister's face, and the anger and helplessness she'd felt as the situation worsened.

''Part of me understood how it happened. Nick Calhoun was smooth. He had his own company, and turned Karlie's head with his sweet talk and his expensive clothes. But beneath his smooth outer layer was a frighteningly hard edge. I suppose Karlie didn't want to see it. Like so many other women, she wanted a fairy tale. If you think about it, a lot of fairy tales have brutal endings.''

Vince nearly cringed at the bitter echo in her low voice. He heard her take a deep breath before she went on. ''Nick never married her, and he left her just before the baby was born. Secretly, I was relieved. I was with her through the surgery when Casey was born. Since Karlie was unconscious, I was the first person to hold him. But Nick came back the next day. I begged Karlie to come with me. By then, I think she was afraid of him. Since there was nothing I could do, I went back to California. Alone.''

''You didn't take the baby with you then?'' he asked.

''No. Although she was afraid of Nick, Karlie was a wonderful mother. When we were growing up, I'd always been the stronger sister. That year, Karlie proved her own strength.''

Her voice faded, then died away.

Vince didn't know what he'd expected, but it hadn't been this. He'd been afraid LeAnna was going to tell him she was leaving, without an explanation, without a backward glance. Instead, she was sharing a piece of her soul with him.

He turned his head so that he could look into her eyes. She blinked, as if holding her raw emotions in check. When her voice came again, it was deeper, throatier, and so sad he ached.

"One night the phone rang. I recognized my grandmother's voice on the other end, yet she sounded strange. 'Karlie's dying. LeAnna, can you come home?' It was the first time I'd ever heard Grandma cry."

Pain. It was a dark emotion, like black smoke. It stung your eyes, parched your lips and burned your throat. Pain was one thing people avoided, yet there it was in LeAnna's voice, and in her eyes. Vince would have done anything to take it away.

"Did you get home in time?" he asked quietly.

She nodded. "Karlie had a brain tumor. It was rapid-growing and inoperable. There was nothing anybody could do. I stayed with her around the clock. Each time she slipped in and out of consciousness, I was terrified it would be the last. She knew she was dying, and told me she was afraid Casey would die, too, if he stayed with Nick. So she signed a letter granting me guardianship."

"Then why are you running?" Vince asked. "If your sister appointed you as Casey's guardian, wouldn't the courts grant you custody?"

"The courts never had the chance. Karlie begged me to bring Casey to her one last time. So, with the letter tucked in my purse, I drove to Nick's house. He'd been drinking, and he lunged for me. He managed to blacken my eye before he stumbled. I hurried into Casey's room. Oh, Vince, if you could have seen him..."

Tears coursed down her cheeks as she continued. "He was dirty. His room reeked of it. He was lying in his crib, tears dried on his face. He was whimpering, too terrified to cry out loud, but too miserable to sleep."

The bastard. It took every ounce of self-restraint Vince possessed to keep from saying the words out loud. What kind of animal treated a baby that way?

"Nick came into the room behind me, saying how he was going to teach the brat a lesson. Toughen him up a little. Vince, Casey hadn't had anything to drink or eat all day. He was barely a year old. I'd planned to take the letter to the authorities first thing in the morning. Seeing Casey, I knew he didn't have until then. By morning, he'd have been dead. So I picked him up and ran from the apartment. Nick was furious, but in his state, he was too clumsy to catch me."

Vince brought both hands to LeAnna's face, smoothing her tears away with the pads of his fingers. "Did you take Casey to see your sister?" he whispered.

She shook her head. "I didn't dare. Nick screamed that he'd find me and kill me, if it took forever. So, instead of taking Casey to the hospital, I contacted my grandmother. She explained everything, and held Karlie's hand, until she died the next day."

"And now you can't send for your grandmother, because Nick could follow her straight to you and Casey," Vince finished for her.

LeAnna took a deep breath. With the strength and conviction that were such an integral part of her personality, she said, "I worked in the emergency room in a hospital in L.A. I saw a lot of victims of gunfights, but I've never seen anyone as crazed as Nick was the last time I saw him."

She captured Vince's eyes with hers, and captured his heart with her next words. "For a brief time, I harbored the fantasy that Casey and I could stay here. You know I love you. But I think we both know I can't stay."

Her words rang through his mind, increasing the sense of foreboding churning the acid in his stomach. "I'm a cop, LeAnna. I'll help you keep Casey safe."

"We can't guarantee that, Vince. You know we can't. Neither of us can be with him every second of every day of his life. As much as I want to stay, I can't risk it."

So, Vince thought, this was it. She was going to leave, just like everyone else. He'd finally fallen in love, and dammit, he didn't want it to end.

Before LeAnna's eyes, Vince's chin came up and his shoulders went back. It was that touch of arrogance that made him the man he was. It made her smile, albeit sadly.

Thunder rumbled in the distance. The sound matched Vince's voice as he said, "That's it? You're just going to drive out of town and never come back?"

Her eyes clung to his, analyzing his expression. Suddenly, she felt her heart quaver as she said, "I'd like to come back someday. When it's safe."

His surprise was evident on his face. His brows went up, his lips parted. Slowly, his expression changed. The corner of his mouth rose slightly, only to break out into a full-fledged grin. "I'll be waiting."

"What if you find someone else?" she asked seriously.

He continued to smile down at her. "I guess you're just going to have to trust me on this one, won't you?"

With that, he wrapped his arms around her and swung her off her feet. LeAnna tipped her head back, watching the branches spin overhead. She laughed out loud, the release helping ease the strain of the past hour.

"Oh, Vince. I really do love you."

"And I love you. I've never said that to another woman, LeAnna. Only you." He ended the turn with her still in his arms. Lowering her to the ground slowly, he brought his face close to hers.

She'd never met another man like Vince, and she knew she never would again. Raising her face to his, she met his kiss, exulting in his male strength, his turbulent passion, and the magnitude of her feelings for him.

His hands moved over her back, molding her to his body. She abandoned herself to the moment, to this man. Thunder rumbled again, closer this time. Her lips left Vince's, but she didn't step out of his embrace. "I'm going to have to leave Millerton soon," she whispered against his neck. "But we still have tonight."

She felt him take a shuddering breath as he tried to get himself under control. "I'm on duty until eleven. Will you wait for me until then?"

She stepped away from him, clasping his hand in hers. "I'll wait as long as I have to, Vince."

"So will I."

She nearly cried, but smiled instead.

"Come on," he said huskily. "I'll walk you home."

They'd made it as far as his driveway when a message came over his patrol car's radio. Vince reached inside the open window and answered the call.

Even with the static, LeAnna heard the dispatcher's message. Vince had to go check out someone's call. She watched as Vince hung up the radio. Tipping her head to one side, she said, "It looks as if the rain is going to water your new bushes. I can't wait to see how big they grow. I'll see you at eleven."

He kissed her once more. It was hard and demanding. LeAnna nearly melted at his feet just as thunder rumbled again. "I'd better get going," she said. "Or I'm going to get drenched before I make it home."

She hurried away from him, down his driveway and over the sidewalk out front. Of their own volition, her steps carried her over the shortcut, around a row of pine trees and through Mr. Fergusson's yard. It was then that she remembered Casey's wagon. She'd used it to cart those flowering shrubs over to Vince's, but had forgotten all about it in her hurry to beat the storm. She'd told Vince she wouldn't be able to take it with her when she and Casey left Millerton.

Smiling to herself, she thought Vince would take good care of it until they returned.

As she neared her own yard, she noticed that the door was open. She remembered telling Rusty he could go back for his motorcycle magazine if he wanted to. He must have taken Casey with him and forgotten to close the door.

With Vince's kisses still on her lips, and his words of love filling her mind, she practically floated over the small backyard. Her foot touched the first step just as the first raindrop fell from the sky.

She opened the screen door and slipped inside. "Rusty!" she called. "I'm back!"

The door banged shut behind her. "It's nice of you to show up, LeAnna. I don't know who Rusty is, but he ain't here. Looks like this is going to be a private party."

Her stomach knotted as she stared into the gloomy shadows of her small kitchen. Her eyes didn't need to adjust to the light for LeAnna to know who had spoken. She'd recognize that gravelly voice anywhere. After all, it was the same voice she'd heard in her worst nightmares.

"Nick."

Chapter Ten

"It was nice of you to get in that little accident." Nick sneered as he snapped on the light.

LeAnna's blood drained from her face, and her heart all but stopped beating. Feeling like a deer trapped in the glare of headlights, she fought the suffocating sensation that tightened her throat, and glanced sideways at Nick. He'd cut his hair, but he still had a beard. Even in the dimly lit room, his eyes looked crazed.

"It took a while, but I finally found you, didn't I?"

She was unwilling to face him, yet she couldn't turn away. She wanted this to be a bad dream, but knew it was too frightening to be anything but real.

Nick moved closer, and LeAnna had to force herself not to flinch. Where was Casey? She'd die before she let Nick have him. With no weapon, she was afraid that was exactly what would happen.

"Seems to me you have something that's mine," Nick taunted.

LeAnna forced herself to remain rational. Nick didn't know where Casey was. That meant Rusty still had him at his house. He was safe, for now.

In her mind, she gauged the distance to the front door. Maybe, if she threw a kitchen chair, she could make it to the living room and unlock the front door before Nick caught her. "Don't even think about running, LeAnna," Nick growled as he pressed something cold and hard against her ribs.

She wanted to cry out, to scream in sheer terror. He had a gun. In her mind she saw how she must look, standing there in terror, a gun jutting into her side. She wanted to yell at him to stop, but she didn't dare do anything that would provoke him to pull the trigger, although she wasn't sure he wouldn't do it anyway. Casey's image appeared in her mind, and she realized she had to keep her wits about her. For his sake, she had to remain completely coherent.

She hadn't closed the door tight when she walked into the kitchen. Now, rain was hitting the screen, dripping onto the kitchen floor.

Think, LeAnna. Think. She had to get Nick talking, keep him talking until she could figure out what to do. Eyeing the puddle of water on the floor, she began. "I locked the door. How did you get in here?" she asked, ashamed that her voice shook so violently.

He released some of the pressure against her ribs. "That lock was easy to pick. Didn't anyone ever tell you that locks only keep out the honest people?"

He ran his finger up the side of her arm suggestively. LeAnna nearly retched. He caught her involuntary shudder, and encircled her arm with his fingers. "Where's my kid?"

She bit her lip to keep from crying out in pain as he pulled her arm behind her back. "He's not here," she whispered.

"I know that. I had a little look around before you came in. Now where is he?"

"Nick, leave him alone. You don't care about him. Let him be."

He loosened his hold on her arm, but he didn't let go. She nearly strangled on her own breath as she felt the barrel of his gun trail up and down her back. He dragged her with him to the kitchen sink and swept his hand across the counter, brushing the glasses and dishes onto the floor, just to make a point. LeAnna closed her eyes as glass shattered at their feet.

"He's mine. And I keep what's mine."

From somewhere, an idea formed in her mind. She grasped it like a lifeline. She needed time. Time to plan, time to escape. She'd do anything for that time—beg, borrow or steal.

Nick fit his body close to hers. LeAnna's throat ached with the need to shout her repulsion. Instead, she took a shuddering breath and tried to find her voice. "Was that you in Kentucky?" she asked, remembering the night, months ago, when she'd heard a noise. Without a moment's delay, she'd grabbed Casey and a few of his belongings and run out the other door.

"Yeah. That was me. I missed you by about three minutes that time. I was mad as hell at first. But then I got to thinking. You might have been smart, but I'm smarter. After all, the chase has been half the fun."

He really had gone crazy. She willed herself not to choke on her words as she said, "You're smart, all right, Nick. I thought you'd caught us for sure in Pennsylvania."

One thing Nick Calhoun had always liked to do was talk about himself. Tonight was no exception. He eased the pressure on LeAnna's arm, and pulled her away from the window. He turned her to face him, but he didn't lay down his gun. He began to talk, taking pleasure in the horrid details of his quest to find her and Casey. Inwardly, she shrank with derision from the look in his cold gray eyes. Outwardly, she kept her chin high, and her thoughts trained on what she had to do.

The hands on the clock on the kitchen wall seemed to stand still, but her ploy to buy time had worked. She didn't know if it had given her an opportunity to escape, or if it had simply prolonged her agony.

For the second time that day, Vince eased the patrol car into the alley behind the Grady Motel. Other than night shadows and rain, little had changed. The trash cans were still dented, the fence was still dilapidated. Someone had cleaned up the broken glass from the neon sign, but upon questioning, old man Grady still claimed he had no idea who had called the station.

Something didn't feel right about this situation. For some reason, strange thoughts raced through his mind. He'd relied on his instincts several times in the past. And his instincts were standing on end.

Vince strode back out to his car through the pouring rain and cast a look all around. He noted the peeling paint and the sign that said Vacancy. A couple of the windows were lit. His gaze strayed to the corner room. Suddenly he remembered looking at that same window earlier today. That time he'd caught a hazy impression of a bearded man before the drape fell back over the window. Tonight, the room was dark.

A bearded man.

The nagging in the back of his mind was turning into a sharp pain. Maybe it was only his own unease, but he suddenly broke out in a cold sweat.

A bearded man.

He made a call to the station, telling the dispatcher the call from the Grady Motel had been another false alarm.

"Your shift's over," the dispatcher returned. "Come on in."

Vince turned the car around and headed for the station. Minutes later, he slammed on the brake and parked the car. He strode in the side door, his unease increasing with every step.

"Hold on," the dispatcher said into the phone. "Don't hang up. He just walked in."

"What's going on?" Vince asked.

"Some kid named Dusty. He's panicked. Says he has to talk to you."

Vince grabbed the headset. "Rusty?"

"Vince! He's got her!" Rusty's voice cracked on the last word.

Fear twisted inside Vince. "LeAnna? Someone has Le-Anna?" he asked.

"LeAnna asked me to watch Casey. She gave me a key and told me I could go over to her place and get a magazine I'd dropped in her yard. I was headed over to get it when I saw a light on in her kitchen. I saw LeAnna in the window. I saw a man, too. He had a beard, and he had ahold of LeAnna's arm. He has a gun, Vince."

A bearded man with a gun.

"Vince, what should I do?"

"Where's Casey right now?" Vince asked.

"I took one look at that man and ducked back behind the hedges. Casey's here at home with me. Vince, he'll kill her. LeAnna told me he would."

Vince felt his adrenaline kick in to high gear. His chest heaved, and his eyes narrowed. "Lock the doors and stay inside the house, Rusty. I'll send a policeman over. Keep Casey quiet. Whatever you do, don't leave that house. I'll take care of the rest."

Vince threw the headset into the dispatcher's hands, saying, "Get me some backup at 513 Maple. And send someone over to 515. There are two terrified boys in that house, and they're home alone."

He literally ran out to the parking lot. Following some inner instinct, he slid into his Mustang and threw the shift lever into first.

He remembered Casey's terror of Todd Miller's beard, and the way he'd woken from his sleep screaming in fear. A baby didn't experience that kind of terror for no reason. At this very moment, that terror was staring LeAnna straight in the face.

Vince's heart beat a hard, steady rhythm as he rounded the first corner, his thoughts narrowing to one focal point. He wasn't about to let the woman he loved die at the hands of a crazed animal.

Hang on, LeAnna. I'm coming. Dear God, hang on.

Nick's voice scraped against LeAnna's nerves like fingernails on a chalkboard. The rain hitting the window didn't help. She didn't know what would. Nick had closed the kitchen door and locked it. There was little hope for escape.

Chief barked from the next yard. LeAnna stiffened, her gaze automatically swinging to the top of the refrigerator. Rusty's motorcycle magazine was still there. That meant he hadn't come back to get it. Yet. She prayed he wouldn't walk through the door with Casey in tow. If he did, it would all be over.

It took her a moment to realize that Nick wasn't talking. Her gaze climbed to his, and she became increasingly uneasy beneath his scrutiny.

"What's the matter, LeAnna? You afraid somebody's gonna bring Casey back any minute?"

"What makes you think that?" she asked, stalling for time.

"Because I know you. You wouldn't leave Casey for long. And I didn't see a car around when I first arrived. That means that whoever has my kid will probably show up with him any time."

"Karlie wanted me to raise Casey, Nick. In reverence to her, can't you honor her wishes?" she begged.

His eyes hardened to slate as he said, "Karlie's dead. And maybe it's just as well. She never let me lay a hand on that brat, no matter how many times I hit her."

LeAnna nearly choked on the rage filling her chest and throat. "I don't know what she ever saw in you in the first place."

She regretted it the moment the words were out. Nick's eyes narrowed, and he cast her a vile look. His fist came up, the impact nearly snapping her head from her neck. Pain splintered through her cheekbone like shards of glass. For a moment, her vision swam. Sheer willpower alone kept her from passing out.

He dragged her body closer to his. "You always were twice the woman your sister was, but you'd never have anything to do with me. Well, now you're gonna pay for that comment."

He half carried, half dragged her through the living room, toward the bedroom. It was all LeAnna could do not to whimper. In her heart, she knew. She'd run out of time.

Karlie, I'm sorry. I'm sorry.

A pounding on the side door stopped Nick in his tracks. In her mind's eye, LeAnna saw Rusty and Casey on the other side. *No!* she screamed inside her head.

The pounding came again, this time louder.

"LeAnna!"

She nearly cried out loud at the sound of Vince's voice. She heard a click, followed immediately by an explosion of sound as Nick fired through the door.

"No!" This time, she knew she'd screamed it out loud. Her lungs burned from the breath she held as she waited to hear Vince's body slump to the ground outside.

No sound came. She closed her eyes in relief.

The wail of a siren drew closer. Within seconds, blue light flashed through the front window, reflecting off the wall. Chief barked frantically, and Nick swore.

He pulled her with him toward the front door. Staying in the shadows, he glanced out the window. LeAnna tried to ignore the excruciating pain in her arm. Gritting her teeth, she glanced at Nick's face. His eyes were darting in every direction, and a muscle twitched beneath his beard.

"Go!" someone yelled.

Wood splintered as the back and side doors burst open. Vince and another officer charged through, pistols aimed. "Vince!" she screamed. It was as if everything were happening in slow motion.

Nick yanked her in front of him. "So," he said, his tone taunting. "You know the policeman, huh? Good. Then he's not going to want to do anything that might get you killed."

He eased backward toward the door. "Unlock it, LeAnna," he commanded. "Or I'll blow your boyfriend away."

With a click, she opened the door.

"Come on, LeAnna. We're going to take a little ride." Keeping her in front of him at all times, he pulled her backward with him out the door and down the steps.

For the first time, she noticed Nick's sports car parked down the street. If she hadn't taken that shortcut home, she would have seen it right away. She might have had enough time to get Casey and run. Now Nick had her. And she knew if she got into his car she'd never get back out alive.

It was pouring now, the rain coming down in a deluge of water. It ran into her eyes and down her neck. Squinting, she saw Vince round one side of the house. The other officer rounded the other.

Nick still had hold of her arm, propelling her backward so fast her feet barely skimmed the ground. She couldn't get into that car with him. She couldn't.

Think, LeAnna. Think.

If only there were some way to divert Nick's attention. Maybe then she'd have a chance to get away. They'd nearly reached the car. LeAnna was nearly out of chances.

Biting her lip against the pain in her shoulder, she went completely limp. Her arm twisted, and pain knifed all the way through her. She felt herself falling, and bit back an anguished cry.

Her dead weight threw Nick off balance, and his hand slipped from her rain-slick arm. She went down to the ground in a heap and quickly rolled away. A shot rang out over her head. She had no idea if Nick was aiming at her or Vince.

Her skirt got tangled up around her knees, but she didn't stop. She climbed to her feet and ran to the protection of an old maple tree.

Moments later, Nick started his car. With tires squealing, he roared away down the street.

"Are you all right?"

She could hear Vince's voice through the pounding in her head, but all she could do was nod.

"I'll be back." He sprinted away, straight to his car. Within seconds, another set of tires squealed away from the curb.

Several more sirens rang through the distance as more police cars took up the chase. The sirens trailed away into thin air as they drove out of hearing distance.

A young policeman helped her inside and settled her into a chair. He brought her a towel and wrapped her in a blanket. But LeAnna knew she'd never be warm until she knew Vince was safe.

Vince eyed the red line on the speedometer, both hands gripping the steering wheel. He'd never pushed his car to its full potential. Until now.

The pavement was wet, and the traffic was sparse for a Saturday night. Nick had run the first red light. Vince had followed him right through. If Nick had half a brain, he'd slow that car of his down. But if he had half a brain, he'd never have laid a hand on LeAnna.

Vince tasted fury. Nick Calhoun wasn't going to get away. If Vince had anything to say about it, the bastard would spend the next hundred years in prison.

His rearview mirror was filled with flashing blue lights. Last time he'd counted, there had been five. Vince was still the closest. Nick was still in the lead.

The rain continued, and Vince wasn't surprised when the red car fishtailed, skimming across the median and heading down a paved side road. Vince downshifted and followed.

Sweat broke out on his brow as he passed the flashing caution signals. He didn't like this road. It was hilly and had several sharp curves. A couple of miles east of town, the road was under construction, where the new highway was coming through. It was treacherous under the best conditions. The rain and high speed could make it deadly.

Vince downshifted around a curve, easing closer to the other vehicle. The police cars were still behind him, and up ahead, Nick's car skittered from one side of the road to the other, nearly out of control.

With his windshield wipers on high, Vince noted the sign warning drivers of the huge S curve ahead. On the second half of the curve, Nick's car began to slide sideways. He took out the Road Closed Ahead sign with his front bumper.

Vince downshifted again. Within seconds, he saw the blur of brake lights up ahead, and heard the screech of tires as Nick's car hurtled straight into a cement barricade. The crash was deafening. Within the blink of an eye, the car exploded in flames.

It was over. Strangely, the knot in Vince's stomach hadn't disappeared. He hated to see anyone die. Even a man like Nick.

One by one, the other police cars pulled up behind Vince. Someone called for a fire truck and the coroner. All Vince wanted to do was turn around and head for LeAnna's. He knew he wouldn't breathe easy until he saw for himself that she and Casey were both unharmed. But he couldn't leave the scene. Statements had to be taken, a report filed.

He watched the car burn, thinking about everything LeAnna and Casey had been through. No wonder she'd been so terrified. No wonder she'd kept secrets. He'd thought his lungs would explode with helplessness when Nick dragged her toward his car. In his mind's eye, he saw the way she'd dropped to the ground and rolled to safety. If she hadn't, she would have been inside that burning car right now. The realization twisted inside him like a jagged blade.

It had been a close call, but at least LeAnna and Casey were alive. He had to keep telling himself it was over. Now they'd never have to leave.

The fire trucks arrived; the flames were extinguished. The coroner's vehicle pulled away, and Vince drove back to the station, where he gave his statement and handed his report to the Chief.

Chief Willis glanced at the report before saying, "You've been putting in a lot of hours, Vince. Why don't you take the next few days off, use up some of the vacation time you have coming."

Vince shrugged and and finally went off duty. It was over, really over. Adrenaline was still pumping through his body as he got into his car and headed for his old place. He had to see for himself that Casey and LeAnna were truly safe. After he did, all he wanted was a dark room, and LeAnna Chadwick in his arms.

Chapter Eleven

It was just after ten o'clock by the time Vince turned onto Maple Street. He hadn't expected the street to be lined with cars. After pulling his Mustang behind the last one, he strode toward his old house, thinking that it looked as if he were going to have to wait a while to get LeAnna alone.

The rain had stopped and the storm had moved on, taking the heat and humidity with it. Vince stepped over puddles in the sidewalk and strode up the front steps. For the first time since he'd known her, he walked through LeAnna's *unlocked* front door.

"Hi, Vince," Mara called. "Come on in."

His left eyebrow rose a fraction when he saw all the people milling around. Trudy McDowell was serving coffee, and Bud, Lettie and Rusty were huddled in a small group, talking. He caught a glimpse of Mike Miller, Mara's husband, and could have sworn he heard old man Fergusson's loud voice in the kitchen. For crying out loud, it looked like a party.

His sister-in-law glanced up from the sofa. "Vince, is everything all right?"

"Bekka, what are you doing here?" he asked.

With some effort, she pushed herself to her feet and cast him a wry grin. "Mara called and asked me to come. You know how she is when someone she cares about is in trouble."

Vince remembered when LeAnna had told him he was lucky to have such a warm extended family, and suddenly he was glad LeAnna had one, too. Right now, he wished they'd *extend* themselves someplace else. He wanted LeAnna to himself.

"Where is she?" he asked.

Bekka tipped her head toward the closed bedroom door. "She just finished rocking Casey to sleep and is laying him down right now."

Vince strode to his old bedroom door and quietly pushed it open. Light spilled into the room, touching upon LeAnna's hair, glinting in her eyes. She sent him a wavering, tremulous smile that nearly buckled his knees. He somehow made it to the crib, although he wasn't sure how. Grasping the side, he peered down at the baby sleeping soundly inside. Casey was lying on his side, one hand tucked beneath his little head, the other clutching the tattered teddy bear Rusty had given him. He swore he'd never felt so much love fill his chest.

Until that moment, he hadn't realized he was holding his breath. He let it all out and took another, whispering, "Rusty did a good job of keeping him hidden."

LeAnna moved closer, placing her smooth hand over his. "Casey didn't even know anything was wrong."

Without taking his eyes off Casey, Vince whispered, "I'm sure you've heard about what happened."

She nodded. "News travels fast in small towns. It's finally over, Vince. You saved my life. Mine and Casey's."

He raised his gaze from the sleeping child, and found LeAnna looking at him. Her clothes smelled like lavender, her hair like scented shampoo. Even slightly damp, it curled in every direction. There were dark smudges beneath her eyes, and a new bruise on her cheekbone. As far as he was concerned, she'd never looked more beautiful.

Vince remembered the fear that had knotted his insides as he watched Nick drag LeAnna to his car. He'd seen the look of horror in her eyes. But she hadn't let fear or pain keep her from doing what she had to do. She'd dropped to the ground, and he'd wanted to cheer. Now all he wanted was to lock his arms around her and never let her go.

Casey made a tiny mewling noise in his sleep. Vince and LeAnna both smiled. They stepped away from the crib, their shadows flickering along the wall like two lovers lost in each other. He brought his hand to her face and twined his fingers through the cool strands of her hair. He traced his fingertip across her lower lip, then brought his own mouth down to hers. She opened her mouth beneath his, and her kiss sang through his veins. This was what he'd needed, this connection, this quiet assurance that she was really unharmed, that she was really his.

LeAnna wrapped her arms around Vince, holding on for dear life. He'd kissed her before, but never like this. His mouth was magic as his large hands fit her against him. She heard voices coming from the kitchen, and realized she recognized each one. In that moment, all was right with the world. Many of the people she loved were right here in this house. Her friends and neighbors were in the kitchen, Casey was sleeping peacefully nearby, and Vince was in her arms.

She smoothed her hands over his damp uniform and kissed him with a hunger that had been born hours ago, when she'd thought she'd never see him again. If she lived to be a hundred, she'd never forget the hope that had surged through her when Vince busted through that door.

From the kitchen, Mara's voice rose in laughter; Bud's hearty guffaw immediately followed. Vince's and LeAnna's lips parted, and she buried her face in his neck, breathing a kiss there. They hadn't said what they wanted to say, but for now, words weren't necessary.

They stepped apart, and he extended his hand. Tears blurred her vision as she placed her hand and her trust in this special man. They both cast another look at Casey before walking from the room. In the kitchen, everyone eyed their clasped hands, then started talking at once. The men wanted to hear about the crash, but Trudy and Mara were more interested in Vince's and LeAnna's joined hands.

Lettie eyed the two shrewdly and, over the others' voices, said, "Come on, everybody. We can hear the details tomorrow. Now it's time to go home and give these young people a little privacy."

Mike Miller laughed out loud, and Rusty and old man Fergusson grinned. Bud clamped his mouth shut, and Mara was struck speechless for the first time in her life. LeAnna smiled at them all, but when her gaze met Lettie's, she tipped her head to one side and said, "You, Lettie Trierweller, are a lot smarter than you give yourself credit for."

Trudy sputtered that nobody would be able to live with her sister now that Lettie's head was permanently swollen. She followed the others down the steps, calling, "Don't forget. I'm opening the diner before church tomorrow, so we can all say goodbye to LeAnna. The coffee and cinnamon rolls will be my treat."

Vince managed to step back a split second before the screen door could hit him in the nose. *Say goodbye to LeAnna?*

He felt LeAnna's arms go around his waist, and closed his eyes as his body responded with need. He'd been cold for hours, and it hadn't been from his wet clothes. This cold came from inside, where worry for LeAnna and Casey had prickled like icy fingers, squeezing the blood from his heart and the air from his lungs.

Little by little, warmth crept through his bloodstream. He smoothed his hands down her back, all thoughts but one flying out of his mind. She was his warmth.

He spread his feet, fitting her more intimately against him. He heard the crinkle of paper, and opened his eyes as LeAnna reached into her pocket, pulling out an envelope. "It's over," she whispered, running her fingers across the plain white envelope. "The nightmare is finally over."

"Is that the letter from your sister?" he asked quietly.

She nodded, and Trudy McDowell's words filtered through his mind. *I'm opening the diner before church tomorrow, so we can all say goodbye to LeAnna.* Realization dawned, and Vince suddenly felt as if a stone had dropped to the pit of his stomach. She still wasn't planning to stay in Millerton.

"So you're going to leave, just like everybody else."

Slowly, she raised her face, her gaze delving his. "I called my grandmother a little while ago. Now that Nick is no longer a threat to Casey's safety, I have to go back to Tennessee. I have to do this legally."

Intellectually, Vince understood everything. But inside, he only understood that LeAnna was leaving. The people he loved had a habit of doing that.

LeAnna felt the change in Vince. Physically, he hadn't moved a muscle, but emotionally, he'd taken a gigantic step away from her. Searching for a plausible explanation, she said, "You understand why I have to leave, don't you? I mean, I'm not only going to petition for legal custody of Casey, I'm going to begin adoption proceedings, too."

Placing her hand on his arm, she asked, "Vince, what's wrong?"

"Wrong?" he asked. "What could possibly be wrong?" He took a few steps away from her before continuing. "A lot has happened tonight. It's been an emotional roller coaster for both of us."

She saw him shiver, and realized he was still wearing his damp clothes. "Vince, you're cold," she whispered.

"Yeah," he answered, in a tone of voice she didn't recognize. "I probably should be going." With that, he strode through the kitchen, straight to the open front door.

That wasn't what she'd meant, not at all. She didn't want Vince to go back to his place. She was leaving first thing in the morning, and tonight would be their last night together until she returned.

Until she returned. Suddenly she realized she hadn't told Vince that she was coming back. Hurrying after him, she called, "I'll only be gone for a few weeks."

Her words stopped him in his tracks. With his hand on the screen door, he turned his head to look at her. "Give me a call when you get back."

Her mouth dropped open, but all she could do was stare at the empty doorway.

"I still can't believe Vince didn't come," Mara declared over the din of the other guests.

LeAnna shrugged her shoulders, her glance trailing to the door for at least the hundredth time in the past hour. Spirits were high in the Millerton Diner. Practically everyone she knew had turned out to tell her goodbye. Everyone except Vince.

Church bells chimed in the distance, calling everyone to the morning services. LeAnna shed a few tears as she hugged Mara and Lettie. On impulse she reached on tiptoe and kissed Rusty's cheek. The blush that rose to his face made her smile through her tears.

"I thought Vince would be here," the boy said quietly.

"I hoped he'd come. But I guess I should have known he wouldn't, when he told me to call him when I get back," she said sadly.

"Yeah, well, Vince always means what he says."

LeAnna rocked back on her heels, thinking about Rusty's words. The boy was right. Vince had told her himself that he always meant what he said. Suddenly she remembered something he'd said last night.

So you're going to leave, just like everybody else.

Other friends captured her attention, but she couldn't get that statement out of her mind. Her heart beat an erratic rhythm as she told everyone goodbye. Within minutes, she and Casey were buckled into the car. LeAnna glanced all around, waving to all her friends and neighbors. There was still no sign of Vince. She started her car, and eased away from the curb. She drove slowly, her thoughts coming one at a time.

She'd always remember the depth of emotion in Vince's voice when he'd said, *I love you,* and she doubted she'd ever forget the lack of it as he'd said, *So you're going to leave, just like everybody else.*

Just like everybody else. Suddenly, she realized that he was afraid that she wouldn't come back. Oh, Vince, she thought, how can I convince you that I will?

She glanced in her rearview mirror, and saw the crowd of people still waving. One man stepped from the curb and walked to the middle of the street.

Vince.

She felt a smile break out on her face as she pressed her foot on the brake. "Come on, Casey, there's something we forgot to do."

Checking for traffic, she did a neat little U-turn and headed back the way she'd come.

Vince had no idea why LeAnna was coming back, but found himself chanting a silent prayer, just in case. He stood to one side of the street, his hands on his hips, watching as she pulled up next to him and rolled down her window.

Her cheek was still swollen, the bruise nearly purple, reminding him of her inner strength and beauty. He was becoming accustomed to the sense of awe he felt every time he saw her, but he didn't know what to make of the mischievous glint in her eyes.

"Are you going to arrest me for making an illegal turn?" she asked coyly.

Vince shook his head, remembering the other times she'd asked that same question, thinking he probably should have arrested her when he had the chance.

"That depends," he finally answered. "Why did you turn around?"

"Because I had to tell you I'm coming back. I happen to love you, Vince Macelli, but I guess you're just going to have to trust me on this one. Besides, I told Casey you're going to be his daddy, and you aren't the only one who always means what he says."

His blood thundered through his ears, and a knot rose to his throat.

"Come on, Vince!" someone in the crowd yelled. "Kiss her goodbye!"

He leaned over, but he didn't kiss her. He eyed Casey, and then glanced into the backseat. Without further delay, he opened the back door.

"Vince, what are you doing?" LeAnna asked.

He turned toward the crowd straining to hear from the sidewalk, his eyes searching for one tall, lanky teenager. He finally found Rusty talking to Ned Thelen's son Travis and Tom O'Malley's daughter, Amanda. It looked as if his neighbor was beginning to fit in after all.

"Rusty!" he called. "Would you keep both yards mowed for me until I get back?"

Rusty gave him a thumbs-up sign, and a cheer went up through the crowd as Vince climbed into the backseat. Turning around in her seat, LeAnna stared wordlessly at him.

"Shall we go?"

"You're coming with us?" she finally asked.

He nodded. Tucking a strand of hair away from her face, he said, "I'm coming with you. I want to meet your grandmother, and see your mountain. And when you stand before a judge petitioning for guardianship of Casey, I want to be standing at your side. When the time's right, I want to adopt him, and marry you."

LeAnna felt tears swim in her eyes, and had to bite her lip to keep it from quivering as she said, "Are you sure about this, Vince?"

He nodded. "You're just going to have to trust me on this one."

Feeling a grin break out on her lips, LeAnna turned around in her seat. She slid the lever into drive, pressed the horn and pulled away from the curb. Meeting Vince's gaze in the mirror, she said, "I trust you, Vince. I think I always have."

"Whuzat?" Casey asked, reaching for Vince's wrist.

Vince slipped his watch over his hand and held it for Casey to see. "This is a small clock. Someday, I'm going to teach you to tell time, and ride a bike, but I'll never lay a hand on you. I promise."

In the mirror, Vince saw a teardrop roll down LeAnna's face. "You're going to be a wonderful father."

He thought so, too.

"Do you want me to turn around and stop by your place for some of your things?" she asked.

He shook his head, his gaze straying from her to Casey and back again. "I have everything I need right here."

"So do I," she whispered.

"So do I," Casey said, mimicking them.

All three of them began to laugh. Casey clapped his hands at his own cleverness, his eyes brimming with happiness, and security, and love.

* * * * *

Take 4 bestselling love stories FREE

Plus get a FREE surprise gift!

Special Limited-time Offer

Mail to Silhouette Reader Service™

3010 Walden Avenue
P.O. Box 1867
Buffalo, N.Y. 14269-1867

YES! Please send me 4 free Silhouette Romance™ novels and my free surprise gift. Then send me 6 brand-new novels every month, which I will receive months before they appear in bookstores. Bill me at the low price of $2.19 each plus 25¢ delivery and applicable sales tax, if any.* That's the complete price and a savings of over 10% off the cover prices—quite a bargain! I understand that accepting the books and gift places me under no obligation ever to buy any books. I can always return a shipment and cancel at any time. Even if I never buy another book from Silhouette, the 4 free books and the surprise gift are mine to keep forever.

215 BPA ANRP

Name	(PLEASE PRINT)	
Address	Apt. No.	
City	State	Zip

This offer is limited to one order per household and not valid to present Silhouette Romance™ subscribers. *Terms and prices are subject to change without notice. Sales tax applicable in N.Y.

USROM-295

©1990 Harlequin Enterprises Limited

HE'S MORE THAN A MAN, HE'S ONE OF OUR

FATHER IN THE MAKING
Marie Ferrarella

Blaine O'Conner had never learned how to be a full-time father—until he found himself in charge of his ten-year-old son. Lucky for him, pretty Bridgette Rafanelli was willing to give him a few badly needed lessons in child rearing. Now Blaine was hoping to teach Bridgette a thing or two about love!

Look for *Father in the Making* in May, from Silhouette Romance.

Fall in love with our Fabulous Fathers!

Silhouette
R O M A N C E™

FF595

Continuing in May from

by
Carolyn Zane

When twin sisters trade places, mischief, mayhem and romance are sure to follow!

You met Erica in UNWILLING WIFE (SR#1063). Now Emily gets a chance to find her perfect man in:

WEEKEND WIFE (SR#1082)

Tyler Newroth needs a wife—just for the weekend. And kindhearted Emily Brant can't tell him no. But she soon finds herself wishing this temporary marriage was for real!

Don't miss this wonderful continuation of the SISTER SWITCH series. Available in May—only from

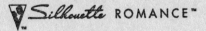

SSD2

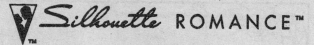

Silhouette ROMANCE™

is proud to present

The spirit of the West—and the magic of romance...Saddle up and get ready to fall in love Western-style with WRANGLERS AND LACE. Starting in May with:

Daddy Was a Cowboy
by Jodi O'Donnell

Jamie Dunn was determined to show Kell Hamilton she was the best ranch hand he'd ever hired. But what would her handsome boss do when he learned she had another full-time career—as a mother?

Wranglers and Lace: Hard to tame—impossible to resist—these cowboys meet their match.

SL-1

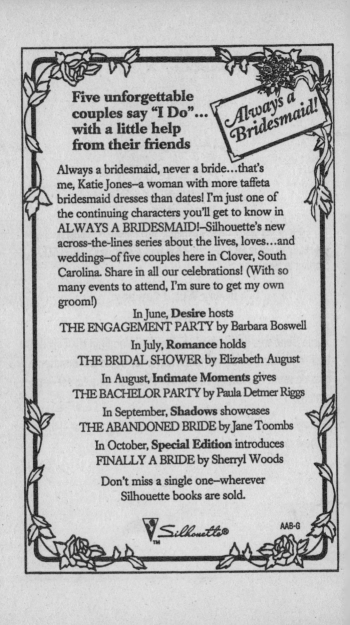

Five unforgettable couples say "I Do"... with a little help from their friends

Always a Bridesmaid!

Always a bridesmaid, never a bride...that's me, Katie Jones—a woman with more taffeta bridesmaid dresses than dates! I'm just one of the continuing characters you'll get to know in ALWAYS A BRIDESMAID!—Silhouette's new across-the-lines series about the lives, loves...and weddings—of five couples here in Clover, South Carolina. Share in all our celebrations! (With so many events to attend, I'm sure to get my own groom!)

In June, **Desire** hosts
THE ENGAGEMENT PARTY by Barbara Boswell

In July, **Romance** holds
THE BRIDAL SHOWER by Elizabeth August

In August, **Intimate Moments** gives
THE BACHELOR PARTY by Paula Detmer Riggs

In September, **Shadows** showcases
THE ABANDONED BRIDE by Jane Toombs

In October, **Special Edition** introduces
FINALLY A BRIDE by Sherryl Woods

Don't miss a single one—wherever Silhouette books are sold.

Silhouette®

AAB-G